A RIDGEWOOD NOVEL

between the
FLAMES

A . R . R O S E

BOOK ONE

Cover Design: KB Barrett Designs

Editor: Virgina Carey

Proofreaders: Nicole Bucciarelli & Kaitlin Keys

eBook ISBN: 979-8-9862673-0-2

Paperback ISBN: 979-8-9862673-1-9

To my Grandma up in Heaven
I know it's strange to dedicate a spicy book to your grandma, but it's
because of her love for old school romance novels with Fabio on the
cover that I even discovered a love for the genre.
Love and miss you.

AUTHORS NOTE

While I prefer for you to go in blind, there are a few situations within Between the Flames that may be considered as triggering for some. Between the Flames is intended for those who are 18+ due to explicit material.

Continue reading if you'd like a warning.

Between the Flames contains scenes with teenage pregnancy, S harassment, and speculation/concern of cheating.

PROLOGUE

Elle

"**E**loise! Sweetheart! Noah is here!" my mom screams over the re-run of *The Price is Right* which is on the highest possible volume setting in our living room. I hardly hear her over the sound of the Plinko chips bouncing down the board and the excited shriek of the woman on TV. This is my every day. My mother always leaves the TV on loud so that she can hear it from wherever she is in the house while she obsessively cleans. The cleaning has become an obsession for her, one that she adopted shortly after she and my father finalized their divorce. A coping mechanism, her therapist called it, but what the therapist didn't know was that it completely took over her life. If my mother wasn't cleaning, she was at work, but the moment she stepped through the threshold of our modest little house tucked in the middle of Shadow Hills suburbia, the cleaning began.

Our house is probably the cleanest house I've ever been in. Like clockwork, she'd arrive home from work, push play on the DVR'd *The Price is Right,* and I'd have to listen to Drew Carey yell "Come on down!" to the next contestant. I miss the days when it was Bob on the TV. He was always my favorite.

As the blood rushes to my head from my oh-so-comfort-able upside-down position of hanging off my bed, I hear the telltale sound of Noah rushing up the stairs as he stomps into my room. A fit of laughter bubbles out of him as he throws open my bedroom door, takes aim with a Nerf gun right at my forehead, and pulls the bright orange trigger. The rubber end of the foam bullet pings me right between the eyes and bounces off, landing on the ground. With a smooth somersault off the back of the bed, I land perfectly at his feet.

Okay, I actually fell into a heap after rolling sideways and falling onto my side, but whatever. Noah is laughing at me so hard I can witness a single tear escape his right eye, and I use his blurred vision to my advantage by shooting my legs out and swinging them hard to sweep him off of his feet. Victory is mine when he comes crashing to the floor in a pile alongside of me.

"You turd," he chuckles. "I totally got you, though!" My eyes roll in defiance as I use my index finger to push my glasses back up the bridge of my nose.

"Yeah, yeah," I drawl, "what do you want to do today?"

It's our last day of summer vacation before we start our freshman year at Shadow Hills High. I'm so nervous that I've felt perpetually nauseated for the last two weeks, and I think I am developing a problem with overactive armpit sweat. That's a thing, right?

"I don't know. My Ma says I have to be home early tonight though. She wants me home for dinner and says I need to get ready for tomorrow. Not sure what I need to get ready for; my backpack is ready to go, and it's not like we have homework already."

I can hear the irritation in his voice. He's tired of his mom treating him like he's still a little kid. I've tried to reason with him, but he doesn't want to hear it. He wants his freedom.

"That's cool." I keep my tone light, not letting my indifference show. I wish he would be less hard on his mom. She's absolutely amazing. "Why don't we walk down to get some ice cream and go hang out at the park? I feel nauseated again and could use the air."

The word *ice cream* barely left my lips before Noah hopped to his feet and was pulling me to mine, dragging me through my house.

"Mom! We're leaving!" I yell just before the door slams shut behind us. I doubt she heard me over the insufferably loud TV, but it's not uncommon for Noah and I to leave and go walk around the neighborhood.

Our departure wouldn't worry her, so long as we're back before dark. I'm not even sure Mom notices our coming and going most of the time, not when she's so busy scrubbing the already pristine surfaces.

Looping my arm through Noah's, we walk the eight blocks to our favorite ice cream spot and order our usual.

After buying our ice cream, we double back toward my house, stopping at the park. It was still early in the day, but we had it all to ourselves—just the way we liked it. I let my feet drag in the wood chips as I sat on the swing, drifting back and forth, basking in the warmth of the late afternoon sun. I used my spoon to poke at my half melted ice cream, not really interested in finishing it.

Neither of us was saying much, and the sound of the swing's rusty creaking chains filled the air as we lazily glided back and forth. My shoe scuffed on the ground as I slowed to a stop, suddenly feeling uneasy. There was a tension in the air, and my skin prickled, heightening my senses. I glanced over at Noah, and my eyes met his.

"What's up, No?" I ask hesitantly. The look he was giving me sent alarm bells ringing through my brain. He'd never looked at me like this before—something was on his mind.

Without saying a word, he slid off his swing and walked

over to the trash can, tossing the rest of his cone inside. I studied him as he approached me with a conflicted look on his face, opening and closing his mouth twice. Running his long fingers through his sandy brown hair, he stared at the ground and toed at a rock. Everything felt awkward. The urge to do something with my hands compelled me to pick at a piece of lint on my jeans while I waited for the moment to pass.

"Okay. This is going to sound stupid, but I'm just going to spit it out," he finally said, and I felt my heart pick up its pace. I looked up from my lap, meeting his gaze.

"Look Elle, you and I have been friends for, like, what, thirty years now?"

I snorted. Typical Noah, always trying to lighten every situation with a joke.

"It's just that we're about to start high school and neither of us has had our first kiss yet."

My eyes widen, suddenly *terrified* of where he was going with this.

"I don't want to start school without being able to say I've kissed someone. It's stupid, and you don't have to say yes, but I kinda wanted to know if I could kiss you so we can both just say we've been kissed and we don't have to risk kissing the nasty band geek with a face full of zits and spinach in their teeth." Noah had rushed through that so fast, he needed to take a second to breathe, his chest rising and falling in uneven pants. I was frozen in place, unable to respond.

"What do you say, Elle? Can I kiss you?"

I was confident what I was experiencing was an out-of-body experience. I could see Noah standing in front of me, see the pleading look in his eyes and the embarrassment coating his cheeks, but what really took me by surprise is that I could *hear* myself responding, "Yes."

I had just agreed to kiss my best friend.

I.

Just.
Agreed.
To.
Kiss.
My.
Best.
Friend.

Dear brain, next time think things through longer before you agree, okay!? Thanks. Love, Elle.

Noah didn't give me the chance to change my mind before he pulled me up by my arms. He made sure I was stable on my feet before moving his hand to cup the back of my neck. I watched his eyes close, and I inhaled sharply before letting mine flutter shut, waiting with bated breath. My heart beat wildly in my chest as I tried to focus on the erratic thump, rather than what was coming next. I wiped my sweaty palms on the sides of my jeans, fighting to keep my eyes closed as the anticipation threatened to send a wave of anxiousness through my body. Suddenly, I could feel the hotness of Noah's breath, his lips so close to mine that they were practically touching. We both stood still for several seconds and my eyes peeked open, when suddenly he crashed his mouth into mine.

Warmth flooded my body as his tongue traced the seam of my lips. I opened my mouth to let him in, our tongues dancing wildly and our teeth clanging against each other. Instinctually, my head tilted to the side, just as he tilted the same direction, making us lose our already awkward momentum and break apart.

We both instantly used our sleeves to wipe our mouths and looked around everywhere but at each other.

My fingertips floated up to my lips; they felt fuzzy from our kiss and my entire body hummed. Noah had stepped back, but I was positive he could hear my wildly beating heart from where he stood.

My judgment was clouded, full of confusion. I could still feel him everywhere, but my first kiss wasn't at all how I expected it to be.

For starters, I had never imagined my first kiss being with my best friend. I had also never pictured it being so... weird. In the movies, the first kiss is always so romantic, but in real life, in *my* life, it was wet, messy, and over as quickly as it started, lasting no more than three seconds.

I turned my head back to meet his gaze and we both instantly started laughing. Yep, that had just happened. I sat back down on the swing, my hands wrapping around the chains.

"Well, now that we got that over with, let's go get ready to start high school!" Noah said, still laughing. He pulled one of my hands free from the hold on the chain and used it to high five himself. I ripped my hand out of his grasp and stood back up, letting him slip his arm around my shoulders as we walked. Wrapping my arm around his waist, I leaned my head against his side as we fell in step and headed out of the park, back toward my house.

"Elle, what if you meet your high school sweetheart this week and I just stole your first kiss from him?"

I snort at that because we both know how unlikely that is. I'm super shy and sort of an ugly duckling. A nerd in the making. Having my first kiss wasn't in the cards for me for a very, *very* long time. At least it hadn't been until tonight. I punch him lightly in the stomach as I look up at him and roll my eyes.

"C'mon loser, let's race!" I take off running, forcing him to follow or be left in the dust.

CHAPTER ONE

Elle

I was hypnotized by his green eyes, full lips, and dirty blond hair. By the formfitting tee shirts he wore, showcasing his muscles that strained against the fabric and begged to be set free. His smile turned my insides into Jell-O. He radiated confidence, oozed sex, and caught the eye of literally every single female in this godforsaken school.

He wasn't an ordinary crush, but we were definitely a classic cliche.

Ryder Thompson.

Quarterback of the football team. The star of campus. Everyone either wanted to be him, be friends with him, or sleep with him. Unfortunately, I was no exception to that rule. I couldn't stop the reaction my body had every time I saw him. Hell, even when I thought of him. I wanted him so badly and I have wanted him for *years*. Almost four agonizing years, in fact. I vividly remember the first time I saw him, just moments after setting foot on campus the first day of freshman year. Noah had teased me about him possibly stealing a kiss from my high school sweetheart and I scoffed at that, but seeing Ryder had me wondering if maybe such a thing could happen.

Wrong.

I was so wrong.

Ryder never noticed me. How could he? I was the nobody nerd. I would *maybe* be remembered as the editor and photographer for the school newspaper. That's if I'm remembered at all. Most people don't even know me as that. I spend my time either in the computer lab working on articles, or in the darkroom developing photos.

I had yet to catch the attention of many guys, but when it came to Ryder, I was invisible. I might as well have stolen Harry Potter's invisibility cloak and worn it daily, for as little as he noticed me. In fact, the only guy who I knew had taken an interest in me, much to my dismay, was the school's resident playboy and walking talking STD, Tommy.

Tommy also happened to be Ryder's best friend, but so far, that didn't seem to do me any favors. Catching Tommy's attention wasn't something to be proud of either, considering he drooled after any and all females in our high school, including the cafeteria lady. Lucky for me, he was more of a "let her come to me" kind of dude, and as harmless as a fly.

I was pulled abruptly out of my thoughts when Noah tapped me lightly on the back. He pulled the chair out next to me, sinking into it. Clicking to minimize the photo of Ryder that I had pulled up on the screen, my cheeks burned with heat at the feeling of being caught staring. Although I technically had nothing to hide, since it was a photo for the newspaper, I probably shouldn't have been staring at it for as long as I had been. Once the photo was minimized, I pretended to look busy by picking up my pen and staring at my notebook. Noah watched my every move, cocking an eyebrow with a silent question, but thankfully said nothing about my guilty behavior.

"How are you?" he asked, slouching down in his chair. He removed a Reese's out of his backpack and unwrapped it, tossing me his famous sideways grin—the one that made all the girls, except for me, swoon. Noah had been my best friend since we were three and a half when our moms forced us to play together at the park. What they really wanted was a friend for themselves, someone they could drink coffee and gossip with, but they ended up forging a ride or die friendship between the two of us.

"Oh, you know, just trying to think of an angle for this article." I enlarged the webpage again, peering back at Ryder's concentrated face on the screen, admiring his features. Frozen in time, he glanced over his shoulder, smiling at who knows what.

How could I get him to notice me?

My thoughts were running away with me again. Suddenly, I felt a cold and clammy finger brush against my chin before it moved upward toward my bottom lip. I flinched and pulled my body back as he burst out laughing.

"What the hell was that for, Noah?" I scowled, crossing my arms over my chest.

"Just checking to see if the drool had escaped your mouth yet," he said, a knowing look in his eye. "Isn't that article supposed to be in tomorrow's newspaper? Cutting it a little close, huh?"

I rolled my eyes and didn't answer him, silently stewing. As I turned back to the computer in front of me, I heard the door to the computer lab slam, followed by a slur of giggles and the sound of wet kisses enter the room. I whipped my head around, ready to yell at the offenders and remind them that this was a computer lab and not a make-out spot, but before I could, my heart dropped into my stomach. Ryder and Lily, the newspaper's lead photographer, were walking through the lab, mouths connected. Neither of them bothered to see if anyone else was in the room as Ryder fell into a chair in the corner and pulled Lily onto his lap.

Lily was a friend of mine, but I never told her about my devastatingly lame crush on Ryder. There was no way that I could. Not only were they dating, they were *perfect* together. Their relationship was the whole high school quarterback dates the head cheerleader type of romance, except for Lily wasn't a cheerleader. Instead, she was the popular photographer for both the newspaper and the yearbook committee. Gorgeous in a totally understated way, with a curvy body, loose blonde curls, and big blue eyes. She wore stylish, formfitting clothes that showed off her assets. She was friends with everyone, and kind to all the teachers and staff. Everyone adored her—the school's girl-next-door. No one was exactly shocked when she and Ryder became an item.

It had been a few months since that had happened and I still seethed with jealousy, even though I hid it from her.

No one ever suspected that I, Eloise Peters, secretly pined for the love of a boy who I didn't stand a chance with. As far as everyone was concerned, my head was shoved so far into a book, or a computer, that my teenage hormones didn't exist, and that was the way I was going to keep it. At least for these last few months of high school. I'd rather keep people at a distance than let them in. As soon as graduation happened, I was out of this town. The one person I ever let in was Noah. He had been my rock throughout my entire life and the only one to know the real me.

"C'mon, let's get out of here," Noah said under his breath, pulling me out of my chair by my elbow. My heart sank into the pit of my stomach as Lily's giggles filled the air. I quickly gathered my notebook and the various pictures I had sitting in front of me for the article and shoved them into my folder. Noah's tone of voice was sharp, and I was ready to get out of there, too. Pushing the folder into my bag without trying to organize it, I reached to grab the long strap and lifted it over my head to fit across my body. As I turned to leave, my eyes flicked to the corner of the room inadvertently. Jealousy and despair overtook my body, taking in Ryder and Lily's bodies melted together, his mouth fused to hers. As my eyes traveled further up their faces, I gasped as my eyes met Ryder's piercing green ones. His eyes bore straight into me with a heat that made my skin warm.

He's staring at me as he's kissing her. I was frozen, heart thumping wildly in my chest as my mind raced with a thousand thoughts and questions. He was staring at me with a look that I longed to have the ability to read and it made my chest heavy. A smirk pulled at his lips as his kiss continued to devour Lily, yet his eyes refused to unlock from mine. I lifted my chin slightly, not backing down from his gaze.

"Elle." A familiar voice floated into my head and snapped me out of my train of thought, causing me to blink.

"Eloise." The sound of my name being called again came through clearer this time. I turned in the direction the voice came from, finding Noah waiting with one arm firmly placed against the door, while his other arm held the strap of his backpack that was thrown over one shoulder. I could see the anger in his eyes.

"Let's go, *now*," he ordered, his tone sharp as he turned his attention to Ryder, staring him down. Following Noah's line of sight, my eyes reconnected with Ryder's. My stomach dipped as I walked backward, unable to pull my gaze away from him. Lily had come up for air and curled into him, oblivious that his concentration was elsewhere.

I bumped into Noah and he snaked his arm across my shoulders, turning my body with a nudge so that I was walking out of the door ahead of him. I ran my hand down my face in frustration. Sensing Noah following closely behind me, I quickened my pace to get us away.

"Dude's scum," he muttered under his breath, his icy tone

making me shiver. I looked up at him, studying his face as we walked, noting how irritated the situation had made him.

Noah had grown quite gorgeous over the years. His light brown hair had turned dark like mine, but it had flecks of gold from the sun. His milk chocolate eyes and that sideways grin of his made for a deadly combination, one that made all the girls at our school swoon. While the thought of Noah as something other than my best friend may have crossed my mind a time or two over the years, his good looks didn't make me want to drop my panties and ruin the only friendship I've ever known.

We had friend zoned each other years ago and were both perfectly content with that. I wasn't his type, anyway. Sure, I was pretty, but I wore modest clothes and nerdy glasses that were obviously too big for my face—my mom refused to even think about getting me a new pair until it was absolutely necessary. I wasn't the type of girl who had boys lining up at her door, but I also wasn't a complete dud. At least I didn't think I was. I was comfortable in my skin and didn't feel like I was missing anything by not having boyfriends throughout my high school years.

Noah, on the other hand, wasn't your typical guy, and that's what made him so appealing to literally everyone. Despite his looks, Noah wasn't cocky or an asshole; he didn't chase every girl who looked his direction, and he really wasn't a huge partier. Add that all together and it equaled him being a total god to the girls at Shadow Hills High. The best part? He had no idea! He was so content in being in this little bubble with me, completely oblivious to everyone else, that he didn't try to change himself into one of the jocks to "fit in". Noah was a social butterfly who could hang with every group in this school, and he did. The nerds, the goths, the jocks, me. Lucky for me, he preferred the latter. I could always count on him to find me in a crowded room.

Choosing to ignore his comment about Ryder, I removed my arm from his waist and instead looped my arm through his as we continued to move through campus. My mind drifted back to a memory of us as children as I let his body guide mine toward the cafeteria.

Trotting down the white aisle littered with scattered rose petals, he wore a tuxedo, and they had dressed me in a fluffy white tutu dress. He carried a pillow that held two shiny rings on top, secured with a dainty silk ribbon. Throwing crimson rose petals in front of me with a forced smile plastered on my face, the sounds of 'oh how cute' and 'aww' urged me to keep going. Everything had to be perfect. I couldn't trip, couldn't let the smile falter. Noah's older brother was finally getting married, and they had forced us to participate. Ring bearer and flower girl. I should have loved it; being girly, wearing a pretty dress, and having people admire me, but all I really wanted to do was go run around in the field next to it and tumble through the grass. A game of cops and robbers was calling me, and I was itching to take this giant dress off. I was a tomboy through and through, and this was just plain torture.

After the ceremony and what seemed like a hundred million pictures, Noah and I were finally dismissed, free to go run and play. I wasted no time tackling Noah to the ground and shoved my pointer finger into his ribs, pretending it was a gun.

"All right buddy, you're going to jail," I said, between a fit of laughter. "Give me your wrists. I'm going to put your handcuffs on."

Noah shoved his hands behind his back so I could cuff him, but his smile didn't reach his eyes.

I faltered, dropping his hands. "What, do you not want to play?" I questioned. He was really making this game not fun.

He looked down at the ground, a hint of sadness in his tone as he asked me, "Elle, do you wanna get married someday?"

My brows furrowed and my lips pursed as I thought about his question. "Uh...like married, married?!" We were only eleven.

"Yeah, like Tucker and Molly just did. I want to get married. Do you want to marry me, Elle?"

"I mean, I guess so, but not right now. I just want to play and pretend to take you to jail." Why was he asking me these things? Gross.

"Well, not right now, but when we're older like Tucker. Let's make a plan to get married when we're like 26 or something, I dunno."

I considered his words for half a second, then agreed. Anything to get him playing again. "Okay," I said, "but what if we married someone else already?"

"I guess if we married someone else, then we can't marry each other, but if we don't marry someone else, then we will. Deal?" he said, almost so quietly that I had to strain to hear him.

Why was he acting like this? Why did he seem so sad?

"Okay," I chuckled. "Deal, but only if I get to take you to jail now."

With his sideways grin that always made me laugh, he smiled and said, "Okay policeman" before handing me his wrists to pretend to handcuff him.

Loud voices lifted me from the memory as Noah held open one of the double doors for me to enter the cafeteria. Scanning the room, I spotted a table by the window and led the way. As soon as Noah and I slumped into our chairs, I glanced down at my watch.

We had about five minutes before the warning bell rang and fifth period started—English Lit with Mrs. Saunders, which was usually just time spent scrolling through Instagram. Mrs. Saunders was retiring at the end of the year and had reached the point where she just didn't care, so every class was spent reading or watching a movie adaptation of a book. Today we were watching *A Midsummer Night's Dream*, and I had planned to pass the time by brainstorming my way through the article I needed to finish tonight.

Once the movie was playing and the lights were off, I pulled out the mess of papers that I'd shoved into my backpack. I immediately regretted my decision to push them in haphazardly and cringed as I tried to smooth the wrinkles out.

Falling into a daze, I held the paper against my chest when suddenly inspiration struck. I quickly pulled out my favorite pen and my notebook and let the words flow out of me.

———————

I JUMPED when the lights turned back on in the classroom. Finally, lifting my head to find everyone around me was yawning and stretching after being brought back to life after their fifty-minute nap. A huge smile pulled across my face and mentally I high-five myself for lifting the writer's block that had been plaguing me as I looked back down at the notebook in front of me. Not only had I drafted the article about our upcoming big game, but I had revised and completed a second draft that was now ready to be typed and completed.

Gathering all of my belongings, I placed them into my backpack more carefully this time, before standing up to leave. Looking around the room, I laughed when I found Noah still asleep in the next row over. I walked over to him and stood above him at his desk.

"Noah, get up. Time for you to go to Art," I whispered, gently pushing his shoulder to wake him. He shot up straight with a grumble, yawning before rubbing his eyes. I took that as my sign that he would be all right and hurried toward the door, the minute warning bell ringing loudly overhead. I hardly made it two steps before choking on a gasp of air as my eyes connected with my favorite shade of green again.

Ryder.

He was leaning against the lockers directly across from where I stood with his arms crossed over his body, looking relaxed while my heart plummeted into my stomach. My palms began to sweat as his eyes burned directly into mine, setting a fire that coursed through my veins while my whole body came alight under his stare. I bit down on my lower lip, refusing to let him see how he affected me. I had slid under his radar for this long, I didn't dare get on it now. But this was twice in one day. *Why was he here?*

He smirked, and I felt that smirk all the way to my core.

I couldn't do this.

I couldn't breathe.

I wasn't this confident.

I wasn't this girl.

The last bell rang, breaking me out of my trance and reminding me where I was. I narrowed my eyes at him and walked away, leaving him standing there, but leaving me wondering if he finally had noticed me.

CHAPTER TWO

Ryder

I can tell by the way she looks at me that I freak her the hell out. She thinks I don't even know her name, but she is sadly mistaken. Not only do I know her name, but I *see* her. I see the way she hides behind her folders in class. The way she always has her glasses pulled down almost to the tip of her nose while she types in the computer lab. I see the way she clings to that Noah kid as they pass through the quad, and the way her eyes *don't* sparkle for him. She may always be attached to his arm, but the only thing they are is platonic. I watch the way her eyes are constantly darting around looking for something, as she lets him guide her throughout campus.

Is it me she's looking for?

Fuck yeah it is.

She thinks I don't see her, but I do. I see her and I know—I know for a fact, that if I gave her the smallest inch of me, she'd let me take the whole fucking mile. And let me be damn straight here: I'd be giving her a hell of a lot more than just one inch.

I've kept it tight-lipped that I've had a thing for little miss nerd glasses for the better half of our senior year. Not even

Tommy knows, although I almost lost control and punched him in his smug face a few weeks ago when he was going on and on about how sexy her ass looked in the shorts she had on. She had caught his eye, which wasn't difficult to do, and it really fucking pissed me off. It took every ounce of strength I had to keep my composure and not lose my mind in front of everyone in the quad. No one could know about my obsession with the nerd girl; it needed to stay hidden. Everyone sees me and Lily and assumes that we're endgame, but what they don't see is me lying in bed at night, burning a hole into the ceiling and growing half-mast for *her*. Fucking Elle Peters with her dark hair and doe eyes that she hides behind these oversized, ugly ass black-framed glasses. She keeps everything that I want to see hidden behind modest necklines, forcing me to imagine what's beneath. When Lily first became my girlfriend, I thought for sure she was everything that I had wanted, but the more I grew to know her, the more I realized she was the perfect girl—just not the perfect girl for *me*.

Elle makes me wonder, makes me think. Keeps me guessing.

I know damn well that I shouldn't be looking, that I shouldn't fucking care, but here we are: football quarterback and borderline stalker.

A pair of warm arms slither around my waist and the scent of Lily's heavy perfume infiltrates my nostrils. My gaze doesn't shift from the hallway, even though Elle has long since disappeared. I roll my eyes as I turn around to face my girlfriend, but I'm careful that she doesn't see my discontent. I press my lips on the top of her head, playing the part of a dutiful boyfriend. Lily is pretty—no, scratch that, she's gorgeous, but somehow, I still feel like there is something missing. She leaves nothing to the imagination and has offered no mystery when it comes to her personality or her body. Lily was all too happy giving it up to me the same day we had made our relationship official. Luckily for her, she had been born with brains and a talent for photography in addition to her good looks, so there was bound to be a guy out there who would find her to be the total package. Unfortunately for her, that guy wasn't me. I had made up my mind to break things off with her in the next couple of days, before she got too attached, which I feared was already too late. She had a plan for her life and was determined to make me a part of it. I knew it was time to cut ties before it got even harder to do so.

"Hey babe!" Lily squealed, pulling back and tilting her pink glossy lips up toward me. I leaned down and kissed her with instant regret. I fucking *hated* the strawberry-flavored stickiness that coated my lips. Or maybe it was just the fact that I would rather taste Elle's lips.

"Hey," I replied, wiping away the crap on my mouth. I looked down at the back of my hand in disgust at the sticky lip gloss that had transferred and smeared. A long breath escaped me as I wrapped my arm around her shoulders, leading her toward the doors of the building. Our next classes were in the buildings next to each other, and it was an unspoken expectation of hers that I would meet her outside of her chemistry class so we could walk there together.

Just because I wasn't that invested in her didn't mean I wasn't a fucking gentleman.

Opening the door to the art building, a strange feeling overtook my body, and I paused before following Lily inside.

Shaking it off, I continued walking behind her, stopping once we had made it to her classroom. She stood on tiptoes, tilting to reach my mouth for a kiss, but I dodged her lips and gave her a quick peck on the forehead instead.

That pissed her off.

Saying nothing, she turned on her heel and walked into the class, not bothering to glance in my direction again.

As I made my way back toward the building's doors, my

eyes fixated on the door to the darkroom. The need to go inside washed over me and I couldn't explain why I felt compelled to. I knew Lily wasn't in there, and photography wasn't exactly my forte... but I couldn't ignore the voice shouting at me to open the door. I hesitated for only a split second before pulling it open and slipping through.

My eyes took a moment to adjust to the darkness, only illuminated by the harsh red bulbs in the room. A wicked smile pulled at my lips when I zeroed in on the reddened silhouette in the corner, leaning over a developer bath.

How had I sensed that she was in here?

Elle hadn't seen me yet, so I stood silently and simply drank in the sight of her for several minutes. She had no idea how hot she was... how beautiful. She had completely captivated me, stealing my attention over these last few months, my fascination only growing stronger and more primal as the days passed. I couldn't wrap my head around it. I felt mildly guilty as my mind wandered back to the girlfriend that I had just escorted to class, but I pushed it away as I watched Elle glide through the darkroom, clearly in her element.

"You know, monsters like to hide in the dark." I purposely shifted my body so that I was hidden within a shadow and watched as she looked around for the source of the voice she had heard. "You have no idea how beautiful you are. So fucking beautiful."

Elle stopped moving, a half-developed photo hanging from a small set of tongs in her hand, dripping into the container below it. She said nothing, so I continued. She didn't know it was me—the shadows shielded me, and I intended to hide in them to speak my truth.

"I've watched you for a long time. Somehow...you've bewitched me. The only thing I can think of is you, and it fucking drives me insane. I've never wanted anyone as badly as I want you, and I don't even know why. Or how? It's... *ugh*...

maddening. You infuriate me and make my mind go crazy. I don't know what the fuck you've done to me."

Fuck. I've said too much.

Furious at myself for letting that much slip out, I retreated as far back into the shadows as I could, watching Elle move around the table. As she drew closer to where I was standing, I could see the clear image of her face contorting with emotion as I came into her line of sight. A breathless gasp escaped her lips as she slapped her hand to her mouth, taken aback by my presence.

"*Ryder?*" she questioned, voice riddled with confusion and disbelief. She dropped her hand to her side, and I fought against my instinct to reach for it.

Fuck.

Shaking off the tingles that had radiated through me again, I hurried to the door, my hand hovering above the handle.

"You know this is Elle, right? Lily isn't here..."

The beating of my heart ricocheted in my ears as she studied me, seeming to seek any ounce of truth she could pull from me. She thought I had been looking for Lily, but it's as if she was hoping I was here for *her*. Shifting my body to face her, I allowed myself to get lost in the two pools of sparkling blue that were searching mine.

"I stand by what I said," I told her, slipping through the door and letting it close behind me. While I sauntered down the hallway, I shook my head, not believing I just had the balls to admit my attraction to her.

THE REST of the week moved at a painfully slow pace, my boredom and irritation with everyone and everything floating on the surface and threatening to overflow. Elle invaded my thoughts at every waking moment, and now she infiltrated some of my dreams.

As if sensing my anger, Lily was becoming increasingly clingy as the days progressed. I knew I needed to stop prolonging our breakup—I wasn't even sure what was holding me back but I kept up the boyfriend routine of frequent text messages, holding her hand, and walking her to almost every class.

Which is what I was doing now.

We walked in an awkward silence, unbeknownst to her, until we reached her Spanish class. I leaned down and pressed my lips quickly to her cheek, pulling away before she could pull me in for more.

"Adios, babe." I smirked, unsure of why I was still turning on the charm. She is still technically my girlfriend, even though old habits die hard, and I had hopes of staying on good terms with her after we broke up.

Turning to walk away, I glanced over my shoulder, seeing that she was headed to class, fully turning in my tracks as I spotted those fucking nerd glasses. I watched Elle through narrowed eyes as she scanned her surroundings before darting across the street toward the path that led into the woods.

Instinctually, I started moving in the direction that she had headed, hearing Lily's voice calling out after me. I ignored it, not caring that she would wonder why I had gone in the opposite direction of my class. Picking my pace up to a light jog, I quickly reached the corner and could see straight down the path. I had expected to see her, but Elle had disappeared. I gave myself no less than half a second to decide—cross the street and find her or head to class. While I couldn't afford another no show to Auto Shop, I refused to not know what the hell she was doing. Elle wasn't the type of girl to skip class and wander into the woods alone... but then again, maybe that's exactly who she was. How does the saying go? It's always the quiet ones to watch out for.

Screw it.

I crossed the road and headed down the path, my eyes scanning the tree line as I walked. There was no way I would risk not spotting her if she had veered off the path. I walked for a few minutes before stopping and turning around in a slow circle, my hands fisting my hair before I clasped them together behind my head.

Where the fuck was she?

My phone buzzed from inside my pocket and I blew out a breath, reaching to take it out. The vibration pulsated in my hand as I stared down at it, seeing **LILY INCOMING TEXT MESSAGE** light up my screen. I groaned under my breath and I clicked the notification.

Lily: Babe, where'd you go?! Tommy said you never made it to Auto.

Fucking Tommy.

Rolling my eyes, I made a mental note to punch Tommy upside the head when I got to the shop. I couldn't even come up with a good response to explain why I was out here in the woods like a fucking creeper, so I just locked the home screen and slid my phone back into my pocket. As I looked up, I saw a dark wave of hair falling over the side of a backpack at the base of a tree to my left. I smiled to myself.

Found her.

Granting myself permission to stare for a minute, I fell into a trance as I watched the way her hand tapped a pen against her thigh. The movement mesmerized me. I incredibly turned on by the risk of being caught by her. Licking my lips, I made the cursory decision to approach her—it was now or never. My movements were slow and calculated as I carefully avoided stepping on anything that might make a sound. My intent focused on seeing what the good girl did when she was caught.

I rounded the tree she was lying next to and saw that her eyes were closed and her headphones were in. My shoulders sagged in momentary defeat, but another feeling tore through my veins faster than a wildfire. *Anger*.

She was out here in the woods alone, with her eyes closed and her headphones in. She was either an idiot or she just didn't care that she had made herself an easy target if some shady fucker came along. I'll admit that my intentions with Elle weren't of the purest variety, but I liked my women consenting, so lucky for her, it was me who had found her out here.

I kicked the sole of her Chuck Taylor, my arms folding over my chest as I watched closely for her reaction. Laughter roared out of me as she nearly jumped out of her own skin, her big eyes flying open as she yanked her headphones out of her ears. To my surprise, she didn't scream—most girls would have added the scream for the extra drama. It's a shame, I was looking forward to hearing her scream out my name.

"What the hell are you doing?!"

Her words had come out in a slur of panted breaths, forcing me to bite the inside of my cheek as I pictured her panting for a completely different reason. The image of Elle writhing beneath me in bed, fisting the sheets, was one that I couldn't ignore, and a smirk played at the corner of my lips as her eyes raged with fire.

"It's not fucking funny, dude. You scared the shit out of me. What the hell are you doing out here? Wait, did you follow me?"

"Dude?" I chuckled, raising my eyebrow with mock confusion.

Her cheeks reddened under my gaze, but her anger flowed out in waves. I guess I could throw her a bone.

"If you must know, I was looking for a place to chill and roll a blunt." I was lying, but she didn't know me well enough to know that I didn't get high like the rest of the idiots at this school looking for their next thrill. I had actually never touched a drug in my life—too focused on my grades and football. My eyes were on the prize. I was determined to get the hell out of Shadow Hills.

As quickly as fucking possible.

Elle's lips pressed into a thin line as she eyed me thoroughly, assessing my answer. I offered nothing additional; I just kept my focus locked on her, refusing to be the one to break the eye contact. The longer we held each other's stare, the more my body hummed. I never felt more alive than when I was in the presence of this girl. My fingers twitched at my sides, desperate to reach out and touch her, but I refrained.

I had an image to maintain and while I was a lot of things, a cheater wasn't one of them. But when she stood suddenly, pulling her backpack with her and tossing it over one shoulder, a sinking feeling consumed me as she walked away.

Before I could stop myself, I caught her by the arm, stopping her in her tracks. A jolt of electricity burst up my arm and traveled straight to my dick. By the look on her face, I could see that she had felt it too.

Pulling her into me, I pressed my body flush against hers, my front to her back. Relishing in the closeness, I slowly slid my hand up her arm to the base of her throat. The scent of her shampoo, fragrant flowers and coconut, floated above me and made me dizzy with lust. I felt myself harden and pressed into her more, letting her see for herself the effect she had on me.

We both stood immobile, the rhythm of our rising chests moving in unison as I trailed my thumb along her collarbone and moved my fingers to lightly wrap around her neck. Silence in the woods surrounded us, the only sound coming from the heavy breaths escaping our lungs. I could hold her like this forever; the feeling of my hand around her neck and her ass against me was a temptation that clouded my mind.

She shuddered and leaned against me more as I ran my nose along the edge of her ear.

"Elle..." My hand snaked further up her neck and to her chin. The raw desire to tilt her head and capture her lips was as essential as air. She exhaled as I began turning her head to me, and she finally melted into me. My lips hovered above hers as I waited for her silent permission—for her to close the final gap.

"Ryder, I—" she began, but was interrupted when my phone vibrated in my pocket, the sudden vibration causing me to release my grasp on her. Groaning, I reached into my pocket to silence the phone, but that was all that it took for Elle to run.

I should have chased her, but instead I stood there watching her go as the warmth of her body drifted, leaving me cold.

WHEN I FINALLY MADE AN APPEARANCE IN Auto, no one had even noticed that I had been gone. The sounds of tools tinkering with the various parts that had been extracted from old cars echoed through the garage, and the smell of oil assaulted my senses. Tommy sat under a hanging mechanic light, zoned in on his phone. Slipping onto the stool next to him, I forcefully grabbed him by the scruff of the neck and brought him closer to my face.

"Whatever happened to 'bros before hoes,'" I asked, jolting him back as I released my hold. He knew I wasn't actually pissed at him, but the snake ratted me out to Lily.

"Ow, man! C'mon."

"You're lucky my fist didn't just connect to your nose. You're supposed to cover for me, not rat me out."

"Dude, she saw you leave and was freaking out. You know

how she gets. What was I supposed to do? Lie?" A touch of smugness was in his voice.

"YES," I roared. "That is exactly what you're supposed to do."

It suddenly became clear to me that he had now set his sights on Lily. It all made sense. This guy, I swear. If he stopped thinking with his dick for once, he might actually be a worthy friend.

He rubbed the back of his neck, opened and closed his mouth a few times, obviously stalling as he fumbled over his next words.

My body shook with pent up tension and anger as I stood and walked to where I had dropped my backpack. Reaching down to grab it, I tossed it over my shoulder and walked out of the shop before I lost my temper. I'd deal with Tommy later, but right now I was preoccupied with two feelings: anger and lust. Heading left out of Auto Shop, I took the shortcut down to the student parking lot and slid onto the worn-down bench seat in my beat up red Tacoma. With the doors closed and the engine purring, I felt like I could let out the breath that I had been holding. My eyes focused on a thread hanging from the seam of the cracked leather and my mind wandered to back to Elle.

Why had she run like Cinder-fucking-rella at the first opportunity?

I punched my steering wheel and sank further into the seat.

Fuck.

Had I been wrong about her? No, there was no way I had been wrong.

I felt the way her body reacted to my touch; I could *see* it. Just like I could see her. There was no more of her hiding from me, and the sooner I could break up with Lily and lose the noose around my neck, the sooner I could show Elle that she was *mine*.

A devious smile spread across my face as I closed my eyes and leaned my head back, letting the music drown out all of my thoughts.

CHAPTER THREE

Elle

Oh my God. Oh my *freaking* God. What the hell was that?!

Ryder.

In the woods.

About to kiss me?!

There was no freaking way. I pressed the back of my hand to my forehead, testing to see if I had grown feverish. It would explain how I had slipped into some sort of dream state coma situation where my ultimate fantasies ran rampant.

Hello, my name is Eloise Peters, and I'd like to check myself into the lovely mental institution where I clearly belong because there is no way that Ryder just sought me out in the woods and almost kissed me.

... but he had, hadn't he?

I knew Ryder had lied about being in the woods to roll a blunt; smoking wasn't his thing. As far as I knew, he had never touched a drug of any type, and I hated to admit how much I actually knew about a guy I had never spoken to before now. Ryder always stayed sober at all the parties he went to... at least, that's what I had heard. I never actually went to any of the parties, but I was good enough friends with Lily where she had zero filter; no topic was off-limits. Plus, I had been in those woods a thousand times and had never once seen him there. I was certain he had lied, I just wasn't sure what his motives behind the lie were.

Realizing I was standing at the front of the school, lost in thought, I started walking toward the back of campus where my absolute favorite place was: the darkroom. I entered and closed the door tightly behind me, pressing my back against it and giving my eyes a moment to adjust to the dim red glow of the space. With my head resting against the back of the door, I bit down on my lip to keep the smile from creeping up my face, my head still reeling from the events that had just transpired. One minute I was laying in my secret spot in the woods, the place I go to for a little breather and to clear my head, and the next minute I was in Ryder's arms, his hand at my throat and his body pressed against mine. And then... I bolted. I completely panicked, absolutely terrified to stick around and see what would happen next. We had both been so lost in the moment; I knew I wouldn't be able to handle the rejection when he realized it had been *me* he was standing in front of. Well... behind.

Not to mention, he was Lily's freaking boyfriend. I groaned, shame washing over me. I scooted my body from the door to the wall and slid down, situating myself on the floor with my legs straight out in front of me. As I looked around the darkroom, my breath hitched and it dawned on me that there was no escaping him. Every direction I looked, Ryder's face was looking back at me. Photos of him lined the room, hung to dry after being in the series of chemicals. Even the darkroom wasn't a safe space anymore—it was evident that Lily had been in here earlier today. I took in the various versions of him, all in 8X10 form. Ryder in his football uniform, Ryder in his gym clothes on the track, Ryder reaching out to take the camera, Ryder laughing with his friends in the quad. Both hands fisted my hair as frustration bubbled through me and I could feel the tears welling up. I refused to let them fall.

"Lily?" A knock at the door startled me and I scurried to my feet. Recognizing the voice, I pulled the door open and plastered the happiest smile I could force onto my face.

"Hey, No", I said a little too brightly. Noah arched a brow, pulling open the door further to allow for his body to slip inside. "Why are you looking for Lily?"

I had never known for him to seek her out before. I hadn't even realized they spoke.

"Oh, no reason." He shrugged off my question, stepping further into the room and looking around. I didn't press him further, still too wrapped up in my own thoughts. "What are you doing in here? I thought you'd be in Econ."

"I just had a lot on my mind. I decided to skip."

"I'm surprised you didn't go to your tree." A scowl crossed his face as his eyes traveled from photo to photo.

I smiled at his mention of my tree. Sometimes it was easy to forget just how well Noah knew me, never forgetting the littlest of details. I was burning to tell my best friend what had just happened out in the woods, but I knew there was a line that we both never crossed with each other, and this qualified as being over that line.

I shrugged, bending to pick up my backpack. "Do you want to get out of here?"

"Only if we go get some burgers," Noah said, lightly elbowing me in the side. Without fail, Noah always knew how and when to make things better.

I led the way out of the dark room and down the poorly lit hallway of the arts building. The tiles were cracked and chipped and the florescent bulbs were half burnt out, causing an eerie darkness. If it hadn't housed one of my favorite places in this entire town, I would have avoided this building like the plague.

Falling into an old routine, I looped my arm through Noah's and we fell into step as we made our way toward the student parking lot. We had carpooled today, so it made sneaking off campus that much easier. Luck was on our side, and the student lot was as empty as a ghost town. Still, we sprinted down the stairs that lead to the lot, hand in hand, a smile plastered to my face. I double clicked the unlock on my key fob and hopped into the driver's seat of my faded blue sedan. We both burst into a fit of laughter as we slammed our doors.

"Look at us, Bonnie and Clyde," Noah said as he buckled in. His sideways grin radiated happiness as he raked his fingers through his hair, smiling at me.

"Oh yeah, totally, minus the murders."

"There could be murder. I could think of a couple people who would be at the top of a hit list."

I put the car into reverse and pulled out of my assigned parking spot. Our security guard, Mr. Hicks, was nowhere to be seen, but I didn't slow as we hit two sets of speed bumps, my car thudding angrily as I drove over them. Excitement swelled in my chest and I rolled the windows down, sticking my hand out and enjoying the feeling of cool air on my palm.

"Slow down, speed racer, we're in the clear." Noah chuckled as he turned up the radio, flipping through the stations so fast I could hardly hear what song was playing before the next station came to life. I attempted to come up with a witty response, but instead stayed silent for the duration of the half mile to the local burger joint, appropriately named Shadow Hill's Burgers.

"You wanna sit or drive through?" I asked, idling in the middle of the parking lot as I waited for his answer. I turned my head to look at him, drumming my fingers on the steering wheel to the beat of "Can't Stop the Feeling."

"Eh, let's just drive through and head home," he responded, a slight irritation lacing his voice that wasn't there when we left campus. Noah stared at his cell phone, clutching it so tightly his knuckles had turned white. I craned my neck to catch a glimpse of his phone, but couldn't see past his privacy screen protector.

"Who ya talking to?" I asked nonchalantly, pulling into the drive-through. I slowed drastically, hoping he would answer my question before we approached the intercom to order. He didn't.

"WELCOME TO SHADOW HILLS BURGERS, WHAT CAN I GETCHA?!"

"Um hi," I said back to the voice on the intercom, rubbing my now ringing ear. "I'll take a cheeseburger with everything on it, extra pickles, fries, and a half strawberry, half chocolate milkshake. I will also take two double cheeseburgers with no onions, extra cheese, fries, and a vanilla milkshake."

Our order was engrained in my mind; we were creatures of habit when it came to our burgers.

"ALL RIGHT HONEY, WILL THAT BE IT FOR YA?" the voice boomed again, but this time I was quick on my feet and blocked the eardrum assault by putting my hand in front of my ear.

"Yes, thank you." I pulled the car forward, not awaiting instruction to do so. I knew the drill; this was a weekly ritual for the two of us. I stole a glance over at Noah and he was scowling at his phone, brows so furrowed that they were practically one long unibrow. I really wanted to know what was bothering him, but I had a feeling I wasn't going to find out. Noah was usually an open book, but it seemed that this was a secret he wasn't looking to share without a lot of persuasion.

"Seriously, are you okay, Noah?"

"I'm fine." He shoved a $20 bill into my hand to cover the cost of our food.

I made no attempt to exchange pleasantries with the woman at the drive-through window as I handed her the money, took our change, and passed the food to Noah. Placing the milkshakes into the cupholder, I curtly offered the woman a "Thank you" before stepping on the gas and driving straight to Noah's house.

I was annoyed and feeling left in the dark about what was going on inside Noah's head. *But you have a secret too,* I reminded myself, my mind wandering back to my near kiss with Ryder in the woods.

As we pulled up to Noah's ranch-style house, a sense of peace washed over me as I took "my spot" on the street. Noah's house had always been a safe haven for me; a place where I could escape to at any time of day and just be myself. I loved my mom, but sometimes I felt like a guest in my own house—a feeling that I never had when I was at Noah's. The Whitlock home was cozy and always smelled like freshly baked chocolate chip cookies. The moment you stepped through the threshold of their hunter green front door, you were immediately greeted by an antique wooden bench adorned with two throw pillows that Robin, Noah's mom, switched out seasonally. What I loved most about their home is that no matter where you looked, I was present. The Whitlocks had always treated me like an extension of their family. Various photos of Noah and I were placed around the living room, my favorite sweater was still draped across the back of the kitchen chair, left there from two days ago. My black sequined slippers that Noah had bought for me this past Christmas sat under the entryway bench. This house was home to me in every sense of the word, and I absolutely loved to be there.

Throwing the car into park, I shifted my body so that I was staring directly at Noah, assessing him as he continued to stare at his phone. I huffed dramatically, trying to capture his attention, but right now I would probably have more luck catching the attention of a brick wall. I scooped up the bag of food and my milkshake, climbed out of the car, and slammed the door. I heard Noah slam his door behind me, and I rolled my eyes as I pushed open his front door and walked into the house. Not bothering to close the door behind me, I slid my feet into my slippers from under the bench, avoiding the urge to look at Noah as he walked in and slammed the front door behind him. It felt like we were in a fight, and I was growing increasingly irritated at his behavior. I continued to ignore him as I walked to the kitchen and set the bags of burgers down, laying down a couple of napkins before placing my burger and fries on them, before I ripped a big bite out of my burger and preemptively dipped a fry in my ketchup. I ate in silence, growing angrier as the time passed.

Noah finally made his way into the kitchen and sank onto the barstool next to where I stood. I studied him closely; he sure looked like my Noah, with his blue jeans that hung on his hips with just the right amount of sag, a blue and tan plaid flannel, cuffed at the arms and unbuttoned just enough to expose the wife-beater style tank top that was layered beneath it. His hair was a little messy, as always. The only notable difference with this version of Noah was the scowl on his face, his current icy demeanor, and him shutting me out.

"Noah, what's going on? I'm seriously starting to worry."

My blood began to boil as I continued to be ignored. Not pausing to consider my actions, I reached over, yanked the phone out of his hand, and threw it across the room.

After watching the phone land on the couch, he snapped out of his stupor and flew into a fit of rage. He stood and stomped into the living room to retrieve his phone before turning to me with malice in his eyes. I returned his icy glare.

"Seriously? Elle, what the fuck?"

"I'm sorry, Noah, but I'm tired of being ignored. What the hell is going on with you?"

"It's nothing Elle, don't worry about it."

"You have to talk to me eventually, you know. You always feel better after you do," I said matter-of-factly before shoving a fry into my mouth.

"I know," he said. "And I will. Just not right now." He ran his hand through his hair. "Everything is fine. Just trust me, okay?" Pulling his burger out of the grease-stained bag, he began wolfing it down. I watched him eat, wondering if I really knew my best friend as well as I thought I did. We were both keeping secrets, and we all know that secrets are the downfall of any relationship.

CHAPTER FOUR

Ryder

I was in a shit mood, tired of the day-to-day monotony that was this town, and angry that I hadn't seen Elle since our encounter in the woods. I couldn't shake the feeling of her body pressed against mine, and I wanted a re-do. Badly. Had she been thinking about me, too? Was she envisioning the feeling of my hands on her body the way I was?

Fuck. Why did I care?

Powering through the quad, I forced myself to keep my irritation at bay. I couldn't let my mask fall, not when I had an audience of people watching me as I moved through the sea of students and down to the parking lot. I'd had enough for the day and was ready to get the hell out of this place, even if that meant skipping my last two classes. What was the point of being a senior in high school if I didn't act like it from time to time?

Once in my truck, I turned my music up to drown out my own thoughts and let muscle memory kick in to guide me home.

I made it to my house faster than I probably should have, threw my truck into park, and went inside. It was barely two in the afternoon and I would have the house to myself for at least another hour until my sister got off the bus. I took the stairs two at a time and let out a hasty breath as I slammed my bedroom door shut.

In desperate need of music to drown out the noise in my head, I went straight to my speaker and plugged in my iPod to the AUX cable, scrolling the music choices until I found a song that would calm me. After I pushed play and hit shuffle on the device, I sank into my bed and I allowed my eyes to close. The riff of the guitar radiated through the speakers and I slowed my breathing to relax myself. This was my ritual when my mind started to spiral; when the thoughts became too much. I had been doing this routine of laying on my bed and working through various breathing techniques while I listened to loud music for the last five years.

Five years ago, my life went from being average and boring to being fucked up.

Five years ago, my mother caught my father at his office with his pants around his ankles and his secretary on her knees. Within 24 hours of getting caught, my father decided that his secretary's blow jobs were more important than his family and left us. It's a damn good thing I was old enough to make my own cereal at that point because daddy never came back with the milk.

Our life went from shit to shitty to *shittier*, and then with time, my mother realized that she deserved better. She quit crying, pulled herself together, and found a job that she enjoyed. Now, five years later, things feel like how they were before, minus one shitbag father.

The sound of footsteps on the stairs woke me up, a jolt of anxiety drifting through my body before I realized I had dozed off. My sister must have just gotten home. Feeling groggy and irritated, I swung my legs over the bed and stripped out of my clothes as I walked toward the bathroom attached to my bedroom. I cranked the water as hot as it would go, letting it warm slightly before stepping in. As the water cascaded around me, scalding my skin, I watched the steam waft above me. Raking my hands over my face, I paused over my eyes, rubbing them in an attempt to wake up a little. Just as my mood was beginning to improve slightly, I heard my bedroom door slam closed.

"Get out Kelsey, I'm in the shower," I yelled, hoping my voice would carry through the partially cracked bathroom door. My sister loved barging into my room to accost me with questions about my day. It was her attempt to keep our brother-sister bond strong. She was in 8th grade and the thought of me leaving for college soon absolutely terrified her. She had become progressively clingier in the last few months.

"Hey, babe, it's me!" Lily's voice floated through the air as she pushed the bathroom door open so that I could hear her. I didn't bother responding as I continued to scrub the soap suds over my body. My eyes fell shut and took a few deep breaths before turning the water off. After wrapping a damp towel around my waist, I stepped out of my shower, but my feet barely touched the plush bathroom mat before she said four words that every man hated to hear.

"We need to talk."

Groaning, I made a mental checklist of what we could possibly need to talk about and wondered if maybe this was my opportunity to cut ties. The door to my bathroom was wide open, giving me the view of her as she sat on my bed cross-legged. Her hair was down, falling over her shoulders and framing her cleavage, her round tits on display in a pink tank top. She appeared angelic as the sun shone through the window and embraced her in a warm glow. The sight alone should have gotten my dick hard, but sadly, it did nothing.

My attraction to Lily was shadowed by a brown-haired girl with nerd glasses.

"What's up, babe?" I asked, slipping into a pair of navy basketball shorts underneath my towel. My eyes flicked over to her just as she burst into tears. I took my time as I rubbed the towel through my hair, slowly hanging it on the hook before I walked hesitantly to her side and took a seat on the bed. Dread pooled in my chest. Whatever this was, it would not be good.

CHAPTER FIVE

Ryder

Breathe in, breathe out.
Exhale.
Good. Now again.

My therapist's voice rang through my head as I forced the panic down, willing myself to focus on the things that I could control. Breathing. I could control my breathing. I couldn't control whatever Lily was about to say or do.

Breathe in, breathe out.

I draped my arm over Lily's shoulders and pulled her to me, letting her head fall to my chest.

My weakness would not show through, not now, not ever.

My fingers rubbed her back, offering her the comfort she clearly craved as she sobbed. My airways felt as if they were constricting as I fought to force my emotions down.

Exhale. Breathe.

I regained control over the panic that had threatened to rear its ugly head, banishing it as I turned my attention to the girl in my arms. Wet tears fell down my chest and I couldn't stop the eye roll that came so naturally. A wave of guilt hit me no sooner than my eyes had finished rolling. What kind of asshole rolls his eyes as his girlfriend is crying on him?

The kind that almost kissed the hot, nerdy girl in the woods.

Shit.

"Lil..." I started, lightly pushing her body back into a seated position, urging her to speak by tilting her head up from under her chin, but she buried her head into my chest again, her arms wrapping around my waist and squeezing tightly. I could feel her heart thumping against her chest as her body melted into me. I sat frozen, awkwardly patting her back and growing more impatient the longer this went on. The sobs continued to rack her body, expelling noises that sounded like she was gasping for air. My palms began to sweat, and I rubbed them against the material of my shorts.

"I think I'm pregnant." She blew out a shaky breath, pulling away from my body to look at me as I stared at her in shock.

The fuck?

My legs launched me off the bed, and I started pacing the room. Lily's mascara flowed down her cheeks like two dark rivers, her small body shaking as she cradled her knees against her chest from her spot on the edge of the bed.

"What do you mean, you think?" I barked. Her eyes widened.

"I... I don't know for sure, but I think I am. I'm late, Ryder. My period is two weeks late and I'm *never* late." My eyes narrowed as I tried to calculate the time when she could have gotten pregnant. I thought I had been careful, always. "I bought a test, but I haven't taken it yet. I'm so scared, Ryder, so freaking scared. I'm only seventeen! You barely just turned eighteen. We can't be parents. This cannot be happening."

"Okay, so you haven't taken the test yet?" I questioned. If she hadn't taken the test yet, then there was still a chance she wasn't pregnant. We could salvage this.

Shaking her head no, she leaned over, reaching into her purse on the floor. She took out a blue box, shaking it before tossing it onto the bed next to her. I leaned over and picked it up, staring at the box as if it would give me the answer itself. Ripping open the cardboard, I pulled out the pregnancy test, holding it out for Lily to take from me.

"Well, let's find out then."

Silent tears streamed down her face as she grabbed the test out of my hand, her fingers brushing against mine as she did. I looked away, a thousand things running through my mind. She walked to my bathroom and shut the door behind her.

I dropped to the floor, shifting my body so that my back rested against my bed. My fists slammed into the carpet next to me. How could this have happened? I wore a condom every single fucking time, yet here we are. I dug my fingernails into my palms, teeth grinding together as I struggled to maintain my cool.

My entire future raced through my mind: visions of me playing college football, frat parties, college graduation. I could never reach out to a certain girl and make her mine— everything would just evaporate into a cloud of dust. Not this. Not *her*. I already felt a loss I couldn't quite justify.

All of that would be gone if the test came up positive.

I waited for what seemed like hours before she came out of the bathroom, holding the pregnancy test. Her tears had dried up, but her face looked pale as she stared down at the test. I didn't bother moving from my position on the floor, barely glancing over at her as she slid down next to me. Wordlessly, she held the test out to me. I looked down at it, my heart dropping as I read over the word I feared the most. I could feel the tears welling up in my eyes, threatening to spill, but I'd be damned if I let them. Instead, I let the rage take over, and I threw the pregnancy test against the wall, watching as it bounced off and landed near my dresser. Lily flinched and started crying again.

"So what now, Lily?" I asked, doing everything I could to not let venom slip into my words. I squeezed my eyes shut and tried to think rationally. This wasn't her fault, not entirely. It takes two fucking people to create a baby and I wouldn't let this fall on her shoulders alone. She didn't answer me. Instead, she climbed onto my bed and pulled one of my pillows against her body, cradling it.

I never did get a response; she cried for an hour before she finally fell asleep and I was left pacing around my room as the sun set and the crickets outside began to sing.

Breathe in, breathe out.

Exhale.

Good. Now again.

CHAPTER SIX

Elle

Almost a month had passed since our victory against Crestview High, and the buzz surrounding the football team had officially worn down. We were just a few weeks away from winter break and our presidential committee was already decorating the school in festive reds and greens. The hallways were starting to hum with excitement about the almost three weeks off from school we were about to enjoy. There were rumors of parties and meet ups, and the promise of drunken nights and relaxation in friends' basements. I wasn't sure if it was just that I wasn't into it or if I was feeling defeat over the lack of run-ins with Ryder, but I kept my head low going from class to class, counting down the minutes until the days were over.

Having a free period in the middle of my day was both a blessing and a curse. It gave me the chance to work on assignments during the day, which lessened my load in the evenings —but man was it tough to regain motivation to continue my day of classes after taking almost an hour and a half off. I typically fled to the library, which was where I currently was, staring down at a blank notebook, willing my brain to think of something to draft for my essay. I pinched the bridge of my nose in frustration as my eyes blurred from my lack of blinking.

Writer's block was a real pain sometimes.

The faint sound of a door closing from across the building caught my attention, and I took in my surroundings, peering at who else was around, finding myself alone. I reached over to grab my phone as a distraction when suddenly the air went thick with electricity. I could hear footsteps drawing near, but nothing could have prepared me for who it was. My breathing hitched, and I straightened my back as my eyes connected with the shade of green that had begun to haunt me.

He said nothing as he slumped into the chair across from me, leaning back with his arms folded across his chest as if sitting together was the most natural thing in the world.

The only thing I could do was stare at him in shock.

"Tell me, Elle," Ryder spoke softly, leaning forward with his elbows propped against the wooden table. "Why is it that no matter where you seem to be, I find you?"

I felt naked under his gaze. My heart beat wildly in my chest and, although apprehensive, I mimicked his posture and tried to play it cool.

"I'm not sure what you mean, *Ryder*." His name fell off my tongue as smooth as honey, but I tried my best to lace the tone with salt.

"Oh, I think you know exactly what I mean, but I'll be blunt. Why is it that no matter where I am in this piece of shit school, there is a small tug inside me I can't ignore, and when I follow it, it leads me straight to you?"

There was no laughter in his voice; I sensed no sarcasm or mockery. He was serious. I had thought the woods were a one-off, but he just put it into words. He was as drawn to me as I was to him.

I stared at him completely at a loss for words. The air surrounding us crackled and I could feel the sparks jolting through my body, straight to my heart and my core. I would be putty in this guy's hands if I wasn't careful, and he knew it. Shifting in my seat, I recrossed my legs, clenching my thighs together.

He smirked knowingly.

"I don't know what you're talking about." I held my head high as I played ignorant. I was choosing to guard my heart and protect my friendship with Lily. Speaking of... "Where's your girlfriend, Ryder?"

A flash of irritation coated his eyes before disappearing, leaving me wondering if that question had bothered him or if I was projecting to bury my guilt. He sat his hand down on the table less than an inch away from mine, and I fought the urge to reach over and touch him. Instead, I stared down at the largeness of his hand, studying the masculinity of his freaking *hand*, and blew out a breath to steady myself. Even his hand was attractive to me.

I was unprepared for everything that I felt when I was around him. The magnetic pull was too strong for someone I hardly had more than two conversations with in my entire high school career, but somehow, I couldn't separate the logic with the lust. This was lust, wasn't it?

It felt stronger than that.

"Look at me."

I fought the need to do as he asked.

"Elle..." he rasped, lacing his pinky with mine. My eyes snapped to his, a whimper escaping my traitorous lips.

"Do you feel it too?" I asked, my voice shaking. I was fighting back tears, the magnetism too much for my brain to understand and process.

"Yeah."

Pulling my eyes away from his, I stared down at a divot in

the table's wood, unsure of where to go from here. So much had been conveyed with so little of words; my mind was reeling with questions that I wanted to ask while my heart was begging to be guarded. I pulled my hand out of Ryder's grasp, breaking the contact, hoping it would clear the fog my mind had formed.

Just as I found the courage to ask the most important question I could muster, the bell rang, and I watched as Ryder stood from his chair. He offered me a fleeting look filled with hope just before he slipped between bookshelves and disappeared from view, leaving me with an even bigger ache in my heart than what was there before.

SHADOW HILLS HIGH'S main building housed all the core academic classes; English, Sciences, Math, and History were all under one roof of the school's three level building. The basement was small, only four classrooms were down there, all history classes.

I started down the staircase toward AP History, but my footsteps slowed as the sound of whispers grew closer to me. I was early for my class. It was still lunch and most kids were in the cafeteria or the quad, so the sudden company had me confused. As I quietly inched down the stairs, I peeked around the corner and caught sight of Noah. I relaxed and was about to hurl myself down the remaining three steps when he shifted slightly and Lily's tiny frame came into view. Her back was against the locker and Noah was caging her in with his right hand propped against the locker behind her. I couldn't make out what they were whispering about, but I stared with a bit of shock and confusion at the fact that Noah and Lily were down in the basement together. I didn't realize that they talked outside of the few times we all chatted together in the hallways or the times when Noah had shown up at my house when Lily and I were racing to put finishing touches on an article that needed to be published. This conversation didn't look like friendly chit chat in passing, so I stayed hidden and watched, trying to make out any words I could hear, feeling mildly guilty about eavesdropping, but not enough to walk away.

"I thought you were going to break up with him, Lils. What the fuck?" Noah hissed, likely more loudly than intended. I watched as Lily's head bowed and she stared at the ground.

Lils? He had a nickname for her?

"It's not that simple anymore, Noah," Lily responded somberly. "Things between Ryder and I have changed, and I can't do this anymore. I like you and I know I said I would end things after the game, but it's just not going to happen now. I'm sorry, but nothing will change that."

My hand flew to cover my mouth as I watched Noah slam his fist against the blue painted metal of the locker next to him. I couldn't avoid the gasp that escaped me at the sudden bang, and I pushed my hand tighter against my lips, praying they didn't hear me. Pushing my body against the locker, I strained to hear the rest of their conversation.

"No, Lily, I don't accept that. You are supposed to be *my* girlfriend. You told me you were done with him."

"I'm so sorry," Lily whispered back to him, her voice filled with sadness. "This thing we had between us can't go any further than it already has Noah. I'm sorry."

"This isn't over, Lily. You haven't even given me my chance yet. I *know* this isn't one-sided—I'll wait as long as it takes."

Noah's heavy footsteps pounded toward the stairs, so I spun on my heel and ran as fast as my legs could carry me before darting around the corner and out of view. As the basement door slammed shut, Lily began to sob.

The bell for class startled me and I counted to thirty in my head before I turned to head down the stairs again. This time when I rounded the corner, the basement was empty—Lily was gone.

Pulling open the door for classroom 3B, I sank into my desk and took my history binder out of my bag. As classmates poured into the classroom, I kept my eyes trained on the blank lined paper in front of me, replaying the conversation in my head.

"I thought you were going to break up with him, Lils," Noah had said.

Noah and Lily? How long had that been a thing, right under my nose?

She was going to leave Ryder? For Noah?

She was *cheating* on Ryder? With Noah?

Why had neither of them confided in me? I thought, and I couldn't help the sense of betrayal I felt.

"Things between Ryder and I have changed." She had told him. *What things?* At school, they seemed the same, at least from an outsider's perspective. She hadn't confided in me about anything in their relationship though, which I guess was for the better, since I really didn't want to hear those details. I just couldn't wrap my head around the entire exchange between Noah and Lily. Shocked was an understatement.

Mr. Coleman walked in and slammed the textbook down on his desk, signaling that he was about the begin his lecturing. I forced myself to listen and take notes about what he was saying, even though my thoughts were everywhere else but the lesson.

It seemed like it had been an eternity before the dismissal bell finally rang. The class immediately ignored Coleman, who was still lecturing, and threw their things into their backpacks. I wasn't in a huge hurry to rush to my next class. I had purposely dressed prepared for PE today, so I wouldn't have to rush to the locker room to change. I was more than happy to avoid the locker room full of stuck-up girls who used PE to "stretch" in front of the guys and flirt with the coach. Carefully, I packed my belongings and headed out of the basement toward the gymnasium to check in with Mr. O'Connor.

The weather was cool and crisp, perfect for running track, and I was ready to let the adrenaline take over and fog my mind into nothingness. I ran in my favorite cropped sweatshirt and yoga pants and knew that despite the cold, I would soon be warm, relishing in the fact that I could put on my headphones, turn up some Lady Gaga, and just zone out. After checking in, I walked to the corner of the gym to stretch my legs out for a minute before catching Mr. O'Connor's eye and signaling that I was headed out to the track. He threw me the OK symbol as I pushed the double doors open. As I put in my headphones one at a time, my eyes scanned the track around the football field to see who else was out there.

I was alone.

I took off running and the second my feet hit the soft squish of the track, I felt my inner peace wash over me. Pushing myself, I sprinted the long portion of the track and jogged the short. About four laps into my workout, movement caught my eye, and I saw a glimpse of someone at the corner of the bleachers. My glasses were in my backpack inside the gym, so the person was nothing more than a blur. As I jogged, I kept my eyes trained on the figure and my heart skipped when the person came into focus.

Ryder.

He was staring at me but made no move to come down the bleachers to speak to me. I didn't dare stop jogging, feeling his eyes on me as I rounded the edge of the track. When I finally convinced myself to turn back toward the bleachers, he was gone.

I slowed to a complete stop and put my hands on my legs to steady myself while I caught my breath.

My heart refused to slow, thumping wildly in my chest as I let myself wonder where he had gone.

CHAPTER SEVEN

Elle

A few days later, I caught up with Noah in the cafeteria during lunch, where he was sitting alone at a table in the corner, closest to the window. He held a sloppy joe in one hand and was shoveling steak fries in his mouth with the other, a bottle of Sprite sitting in front of him with the cap already off. I shrugged out of my zip up hoodie and sat down, pulling my bagged lunch from my book bag. I couldn't stand the cafeteria food. The only good thing they offered were the fresh baked chocolate chip cookies, and I really needed to cut back on those; one a day was starting to catch up with me. I nibbled at my egg salad, looking out the window that faced the Language Village and Auto Shop.

"I got into San Francisco State," Noah nonchalantly said while chewing on a mouthful of sloppy joe. "Early acceptance."

"Noah, that's freaking awesome!"

I was trying not to think about my college applications. I had only applied to the best of the best and my safety school was still a hard one to get into. My grades were near perfect, but the unknown had my anxiety through the roof. Noah shrugged and went back to not talking. I used the silence to scroll through Instagram, letting the stories play while I mindlessly clicked through them.

Suddenly, my skin prickled. I glanced at Noah to find his eyes glued across the room. Following his line of sight, my gaze fell on Ryder, who was already watching me. I inhaled sharply as his eyes searched my face, his features softening. The sleeves of his shirt were rolled to his elbows, his arm draped across the back of Lily's chair as she chatted with the girl beside her.

"I fucking hate that guy," Noah mumbled under his breath.

"What happened with Lily a few days ago?" I asked, keeping my gaze on Ryder. "I saw you guys in the basement... I'm sorry, I wasn't trying to listen in. Okay, maybe I was. Look, I saw you punch the locker next to her. And before you even try to lie to me, I know something's up, No. I'm not stupid."

He groaned and from the corner of my eye, I saw him rub his hand over his face before turning to the window.

"Not much to tell. We've been talking for a couple months now, hanging out in groups. I thought it could go somewhere. She said she wanted to be with me, but now she's decided to stay with Ryder. Says shits changed."

I turned to him, watching as he shrugged, trying to play it cool, but I could see that he was hurting. Reaching over, I took his hand in mine.

The bell rang, signaling that lunch was over, but neither one of us seemed in a hurry to get to our next classes. We sat hand in hand, staring out the window as kids scurried out of the building, backpacks slung over their backs, some of them holding hands with their boyfriends and girlfriends. The one-minute bell finally motivated me to stand up, pushing the chair out behind me as I did. Noah made no effort to stand.

"Burgers after school?"

Noah nodded his head yes, and I offered another small smile. "Okay, I'll meet you at the car later."

Shrugging my backpack onto my shoulders, I walked toward the double doors, stopping to look over my shoulder at Noah one last time. He was staring down at his phone, a blank expression on his face. With a deep sigh, I continued through the doors and headed across the quad toward my class. I managed to slip into my seat just as the late bell rang.

I WAS BORED TO TEARS, staring at the clock, watching every passing second. With forty-five minutes left of class, I feared I was going to fall asleep. Excusing myself to go to the bathroom, I shut the classroom door quietly behind me before leaning against the wall for several seconds. The girls' bathroom wasn't far, so I took my time, walking slowly and letting my fingertips glide over the coolness of the metal lockers that lined the hallways. I rounded the corner before stopping dead in my tracks, seeing Ryder with a small group of friends circled together near one of the empty classrooms. They spoke in hushed tones, my presence unnoticed. I shook out of my stupor and continued toward the girls' room, sliding my phone out of my back pocket to give my attention to. My feet carried me past their group and I exhaled as I rounded another corner and out of their sight. I had barely made it another step before hearing his voice.

"I'll catch you later, guys."

I quickened my pace, but it was no use as the warmth of his hand gripped my wrist and forced me to stop walking.

"Elle."

My heart felt like it was a ping-pong ball being batted at with him on both sides. I couldn't deny that there was something between us; the feeling I have every time I'm in his presence proved that, but these last few weeks had shown me that it was just a thrill for him. Something new and exhilarating. I craved a chance with him, to see if this could go somewhere, but he was showing me every day that he stayed with Lily, that he wasn't choosing me. It was time for me to protect my heart, because it was feeling weaker and weaker every time he sought me out. I mustered every ounce of courage that I had in my body and looked him straight in the eyes, my stare unwavering as I told him my peace.

"Elle, please," he whispered, as if he could predict what I was about to say.

"No, Ryder. Stop, just stop. You don't even know me. Until recently, you didn't even know I existed. I don't know what your sudden fascination with me is, but I've liked you for so long... whatever you're doing, whatever this—," I gestured between us, "is, it's not fair. *You're* not being fair. You have a girlfriend. So just please. If this is just a game for you, I want nothing to do with it. The way I feel about you is not a joke, Ryder. Not like your sudden obsession with me is."

I had officially snapped, rage and hurt bubbling over. Ripping my wrist from his grasp, I ran toward the bathroom, pushing the door open and locking myself in the closest stall. A few silent tears slipped as I laid the first layer of brick around my heart.

CHAPTER EIGHT

Elle

As I threw my head back with admiration over the sea of graduation caps being tossed, I couldn't stop the exhale of breath that escaped my lips and the smile that grew across my face. Graduation was here, and I was ready to put this school behind me and start my life. Really, I couldn't wait to get away from the people and drama that this school held within its walls—I was ready to run and to run fast. I looked to my left and saw the smiling faces of the people I was closest to. Next to me, Noah had his fist stretched out into the air, excitement written all over him as a bead of sweat dripped from his hairline down his cheek. In the row in front of me, Lily's swollen pregnant belly stretched far in front of her open graduation gown, a genuine smile across her face—the first I had seen in a while.

The last few months had been a whirlwind. It came out a couple of months after I overheard Noah and Lily in the hall; her telling him she had gotten pregnant by Ryder, without actually telling him.

She had made the decision to keep the baby, and Ryder proposed to her during spring break. With only three months left of school, Ryder had been putting any extra time he had into working construction and saving up for when the baby was born. Although the pregnancy was a shock to everyone, what really shook me was their engagement. That sort of commitment was a nail in the coffin for any hope my traitorous heart had carried.

I think it had broken Noah's heart, too.

We never spoke of it, but for the next several weeks, neither of us had been in the right headspace.

As we rapidly approached the end of the school year, it became time to buckle down, study for our finals, and put more focus on the future. Soon, Noah would be off to San Francisco State and I was headed south to UCLA. I knew in my heart that Noah and I would always be friends, but I was ready for the fresh start I so desperately craved my entire life. It was time for me to get in my car and drive. Just one more week.

First, I needed to make it through tonight's graduation party.

"We did it, Elle! We're finally done with this place!" Noah said, engulfing me in a bear hug and spinning me around. When he sat me down, I laced my arm through his and tilted my head to lie on his arm, taking in the scene around us as graduates posed with happy family members for pictures, accepted bouquets of flowers, and took selfies with friends. The bleachers started to clear out, and I spotted our families waiting for us. Smiling, I gave his arm a tug and led him down to where they were, their arms filled with flowers and signs.

The sun was setting and our families made plans to go out for a celebratory dinner.

"What are my two favorite graduates in the mood for?" Noah's mom, Robin, asked.

As if on cue, my stomach growled loudly and everyone laughed at the timing. We agreed to meet at Maria's Pizza and went our separate ways: Noah's parents and my mom toward the main parking lot and me and Noah toward the student lot.

"I'm so relieved I could cry, No! We're finally done—out of this place!"

"Thank fuck! I can't wait to get wasted tonight and never see these assholes again."

"Okay, drama king, you know you will be at every single party until you move to San Fran, so don't act like you won't ever see anyone again." My cheeks hurt from the smile that had taken root on my face.

"Well, I wouldn't have to agree to go to so many parties to keep busy if someone hadn't decided to move the first chance she got. What else am I supposed to do for half the summer now that you're up and moving so soon?" There was a bit of an edge to his tone; he was still mad about my early departure from Shadow Hills.

There was no use arguing about this for the thousandth time, so I just gave him my 'I'm not even going to respond to that' look and opened my car door. Noah took the hint and followed, climbing into my car. I took a minute to hook my phone to the car audio and put on one of my many playlists: Random Rap. As the beginning notes to "No Diggity" came through the speakers, I turned up the volume as high as I could without blowing them out, and threw my car into reverse. Rolling the windows down, I took a sharp left out of the parking lot, succumbing to the feeling of the vibration of the bass, the sound of squealing tires, and the feeling of the wind harshly blowing in my hair. It was the promise of freedom and fun. I felt giddy as I glanced over at Noah, finding him watching me with a huge smile.

"What?" I yelled over the noise.

"Oh nothing Elle, just engraving this moment into my memory."

I grinned back at my best friend and started rapping the lyrics.

Within five minutes, we pulled into the parking lot of Maria's Pizza, and I pulled into a spot near the back. I was mindful of turning the volume down and rolling up the windows before I climbed out of my car, removing my graduation gown, and tossing it into the back seat before shutting the door. Our families waited for us at the entrance and let us walk in first. As we crossed the threshold of the restaurant, the staff of Maria's starting hooting and clapping for us, along with the other patrons who were enjoying their meals. My cheeks flamed with embarrassment—this town was entirely too small. I awkwardly adjusted my glasses and followed the hostess to a huge booth in the corner. Mindless chit chat ensued until our pizzas and salads were served and we dug in, eating quietly as the hunger took over.

Once the checks had been paid and the goodbyes had been said, Noah leaned over, kissed me on the cheek and told me to go get ready for our graduation party; he would be picking me up in about an hour.

As I drove home, my thoughts drifted to Ryder and the look on his face when he threw his graduation cap into the air; his mask had slipped and I could see the sorrow he was feeling written all over him like words on a page of my favorite book. Engaged and about to be a father at eighteen was a lot to take in, but he was handling it better than some grown men would. My heart weighed heavy knowing that I would never have the chance to explore my feelings with him, but I understood why.

When the pregnancy rumors circulated around social media and a wildfire of text messages, I refused to believe them, insisting that the rumors were just rumors. I stayed strong for Lily, denying and brushing them off, and having her back with the internet trolls. I was certain that she would have told me if she was, and confident that her silence was confirmation that there was no truth to the subject. When we returned to school after the new year, Lily never brought it up, and I never asked.

Within a couple of weeks, I started noticing her style change from trendy tight clothes to those that were looser fitting. I remember the feeling of my stomach sinking with the realization that there might actually be truth to the rumors. Gathering my courage one afternoon, I cornered her outside of the empty computer lab and bluntly asked her if she was pregnant.

With her head hung down, she nodded. Yes.

Instantly, the sadness that surrounded her flooded into me too, and I felt the discontent that she held for herself in that moment. There was nothing I could say to make those feelings lessen, so I did what any decent friend would do and pulled her into a hug. I held her tightly, rubbing my hand up and down her back in a way that I hoped would bring her some comfort. I hoped that my touch would somehow convey the words that I couldn't get out—that I would always be there for her, that I loved her, and that it would be okay.

It was in that hug that I felt the firmness of her stomach as she held me tightly back. It was also in that hug that I felt my heart shatter for her, Ryder, and also for myself.

Ryder could never be mine.

CHAPTER NINE

Ryder

I sat in the crowded room filled with people I had known my entire life, watching them smoke weed and chug their mediocre beer out of Solo cups. Everywhere I looked, couples were intertwined. Some were dancing, some were hooking up, and none of them gave a single shit about being watched. I had never felt more alone, and as I looked down at my shitty beer, the bass pumping through the speakers; I realized that this would probably be the last party I go to for a long time. I scowled at the scene around me, regretting my decision to come. Tommy tried to pass me a blunt, but I pushed his arm away, letting out an angered growl.

"Lighten up, man! This is the time to party it up, get cross faded, and hook up with hot chicks!" he slurred, the effect of the weed and alcohol mixed already taking effect.

Standing, I began to walk away, and a girl I had never seen before fell into my spot on the couch, reaching for the blunt still hanging from Tommy's outstretched hand. Tossing my beer can into the trash, I walked toward the back door, needing to get away from these people and get some air. Outside, the fire pit was roaring, the heat of the flames pulsating in the air and pulling me toward it. As I drew closer, I realized Elle, Noah, and some other kid who I had seen a few times were the ones who had found solitude in the warmth. I stared at Elle as I approached, the glow of the flames dancing across her face, enhancing her features. Quietly, I sat opposite the fire from them, saying nothing and pulling out my phone to make it look like I had something else to concentrate on.

Noah and whatever his name was kept talking as if I hadn't just walked over, but I could feel *her* eyes on me from across the fire. I took pleasure in the feeling of her attention focused on me; it did something to me. It made me feel alive.

The smoke was heavy from the wet wood used when building the fire, but I could clearly see the two pools of crystal blue that were magnified by her nerdy as fuck, hot librarian glasses. Now that I held her gaze, I sure as shit wasn't going to be the one to break the eye contact. With each passing moment, the redness in her cheeks grew and her breathing became uneven.

She was forced to pull her attention when Noah lightly bumped her shoulder. I didn't have to try to eavesdrop on their conversation because he purposely spoke in a heightened tone as he kept a watchful eye on me.

"Is that cool, Elle?" Noah said to her, a look of concern on his face as he looked back at her, waiting for her response. I played indifferent, staying cool and collected as I stared down at my phone, acting as if I wasn't paying attention to them in the slightest.

"Uhhh, is what cool?" she questioned, and I swear she stuttered a little.

"I'm going to go inside and grab another beer with Henry, but I wanted to make sure you were cool." He cast a pointed look in my direction and I knew immediately what he was asking without saying the words. *Would she be okay left alone with me?*

"Uhhh yeah, sure, I'm fine," she told him, her eyes still on me. I followed his movements as he walked away, leaving me and Elle alone by the fire.

The sound of the screen door slamming carried through the air as I studied her between the flames, my foolish heart begging me to make her mine. She was staring down at her hands, her dark hair falling in waves around her shoulders and face. Normally she wore clothes that my mother would approve of, but tonight she was in a dark green dress with a neckline that dipped just the right amount between her cleavage, leaving me wanting to see more. I shifted in my seat to readjust the hard on that had appeared out of nowhere, and continued to watch her, wondering if she'd look back up. If she wouldn't willingly, I knew how I could bring her focus back to me—so I spoke.

"I would have kissed you in the woods that day if you hadn't run away from me," I told her, licking my lips as I remembered the feeling of her soft skin.

That got her attention. My shoulders shook in a silent laugh as I watched the emotions flicker over her face: confusion, sadness, lust. She opened her mouth like she wanted to respond, but I cut her off before she could say anything. If I was going to say this, I needed to say it now, and then I was going to get the fuck away from this party and away from her. I stood and moved to her side of the fire, taking the open seat next to her.

"I know you feel like I've been playing games. You think that this whole time I've had no idea who you are, but you are wrong. I've always seen you, Elle, and always wondered about you. I wanted to talk to you for so long. It took me a long time to realize that I wanted *you* — too long — and when I finally did, I thought how fucking cliche. We are worlds apart. The jock and the nerd." I stopped, realizing that sounded completely dickish. "No offense."

I raked my hand down my face before continuing, so frustrated that I was fucking this up.

"That day I followed you, I had seen you go into the woods and I couldn't stop myself from going after you, if only to see just what it was to make little miss goodie-two-shoes skip a class and sneak off all alone. Then when I saw you laying against the tree, I was overwhelmed by the need to protect you, even though you didn't need my protection. I couldn't just leave you alone and go back. Then I wanted to kiss you, and I was going to, but you took off running. I don't blame you for that, but Elle, you've been in my head every day since *before* then, torturing me. I've denied the pull to you for so long before realizing that I didn't want to deny it anymore. I was going to break up with Lily, but then we found out she was pregnant." I moved out of the chair and crouched down in front of her, even though I had already been close enough. I wanted to be closer. I wanted to touch her. *Needed to.* I could feel my fingers twitch, desperate to reach out, but I didn't.

I was about to be a fucking father.

My stomach sank as I watched her blue eyes fill with tears.

"I'm a man of my word and I will always do what I think is the right thing to do. Lily and I are going to get married, have this baby, and I will give them both the life they deserve. But I didn't want you to leave this town without me telling you that I will always be thinking about the what-if. I needed you to know that I saw... I see you... and I will always be thinking about you."

There was nothing left to say, so I stood and walked away from the girl I could never have a future with, leaving my heart behind with her.

Present Day

CHAPTER TEN

Elle

Ellie Goulding's voice sang through my headphones as I finished up my last hour at work, calming me and guiding me through the final touches of the article I was pushing my deadline for.

"How Long Will I Love You" had been on my playlist for longer than I care to admit, and I have listened to it at least twice every single day since adding it. The first time I heard it, the song took my breath away and tears instantly pooled in my eyes as my mind flooded with the night my heart was ripped from my chest: green eyes staring at me between the flames. His words haunted my dreams and daydreams.

I will always be thinking about the what-if.

The memory of a single tear sliding down my cheek the first time I heard that song made it hard to breathe as I relived it in my thoughts. How could the words of a song speak to my soul so fiercely that all the walls I had spent years building came crumbling down?

The last eight years went by in a slow blur as I went through the motions throughout college, studying hard, partying hard, and pushing myself in order to obtain my degree, but it didn't take more than three semesters before realizing that I had made a mistake. The place that I couldn't get away from was also the place that I couldn't curb my homesickness for, and the second I graduated, I knew I would be heading back. It made me feel both alive and nauseous.

When my time in college had come to an end, I packed my car full of the belongings that I had accumulated, hugged my dorm-mate goodbye, and hit the road. The sensation of déjà vu was strong as I retraced my steps, fleeing from my home yet again, as fast as I could. In the months leading up to my departure, it had become strikingly clear to me that you never know how good you have it until it's gone. The grass is always greener... you get the picture. I missed my family; I missed the comfort of the town I grew up in.

It was time for me to leave.

But at the same time, I knew I couldn't go back to Shadow Hills. There were still things, *people*, I was avoiding. Instead, I made the neighboring city of Ridgewood my new landing place, hoping that this time I could find the contentment that I so greatly craved. I couldn't put my finger on my reasoning for still holding onto a high school infatuation, but no matter what I did to detach my heart, I just couldn't.

When I moved back, it didn't take me long to secure a place to live, thankfully. I quickly found a granny unit to rent on the side of a sweet elderly couple's home and not only fell in love with the space, but the couple too. The Wilsons were in their seventies and had been married for over fifty years. Long term empty nesters, they called themselves, and they were all too happy to rent to me. I was quickly adopted as one of their own and together we loved to spend hours sitting in their garden, sipping on iced tea, while I listened to the stories they told. They referred to me as the granddaughter they never had and were constantly trying to set me up with one of their many grandsons. Although I adored the Wilsons and the opportunity I had been given by them, I was incredibly lonely at times—coming home to an empty studio often had me feeling a little blue after sharing my space with a roommate in the prior years. Despite the loneliness, it seemed that things in my life were finally on track.

It had been five years since moving to Ridgewood, eight years since high school, and I had acquired precisely one friend who I knew would always be my ride or die. I had always been relatively closed off, but I found that the older I became, the less I wanted to put myself out there and make friends.

Rosie, however, is a friend that I am incredibly grateful for. We met in the most of the wall way—literally bumping into each other in the feminine care section at Target. I was perusing the various tampon options, looking for a better brand, and she rounded the corner with a bulk box of condoms in her hand. I quirked a brow at the box while she rolled her eyes at mine, and we both fell into a fit of laughter.

The rest was history.

She was exactly what I needed in my life to balance me out. The storm to my calm. Where I am a little more quiet and reserved, Rosie is rough around the edges and every biker's wet dream. She's tall, slender, and has long, sleek black hair. Her hazel eyes are a little too big for her face, and her lips are full. Rosie's arms are covered in black and gray artwork done by a man named Ramon, and she always wears clothes that reveal just the right amount of cleavage and midriff.

Rosie is everything that I wished I could be more of: confident, outspoken, fierce, and strong. She's a take no prisoners kind of woman who always fights for what she wants and *who* she wants, and she is loud. So loud. In both volume and with her life. She's the yin to my yang and being around her made me feel whole again—*makes* me feel whole again—and I haven't felt whole since I left my friendship with Noah behind all those years ago.

The only thing that didn't really fit her was her name. "Too sweet," she had scoffed shortly after we met, and I had to agree.

ONE COOL DECEMBER AFTERNOON, Rosie and I sat on my couch munching on snack mix, and I watched over her shoulder as she scrolled through Facebook on her phone. She cackled as she peeked at the profiles of people she had gone to school with in the past, passing judgment based on what they posted on their timeline. She continued scrolling, rolling her eyes while giving me the backstory about who was who, who dated who, and revealing the minuscule details she knew about their current lives.

One of her favorite pastimes was Facebook stalking her old boyfriends, lovers, and frenemies.

"Truthfully Elle, you should do a little stalking of your own. It's tons of fun," she said, tossing her phone aside and plucking mine from my hands. "What did you say your old high school crush's name was? Ryan? Ryland?"

Panic seized my heart, clutching it tightly. Nope, no thank you, ma'am, we wouldn't be going there.

"Ummm... I'm good. I don't really want to stalk anyone." I chose my words carefully, not trying to seem like her wanting to look him up affected me. It wasn't like I hadn't Facebook stalked him myself. A girl has curiosities, but it had been a significant amount of time since I had pulled up his profile. Maybe... two years? I was damn proud of that length of time, too. Older and wiser Elle was doing much better than younger and dumber Elle had when she Facebook stalked him more than she'd care to admit.

Had he ever Facebook stalked me?

"Ryder!" Rosie shouted, the proudness thick in her voice that she remembered his name. "Ryder Thomas!"

"Thompson," I gritted through my teeth. I guess this was happening.

Rosie typed his name into the search function, her eyes following the screen as she searched for the correct profile. I'm not sure why she bothered looking when it was clear he was the first one listed. We had mutual friends, but I never friend requested him, and he never requested me. It was better that way. She clicked on his profile and a devious smile inched across her face.

She let out a low whistle. "Wouldn't mind taking this one home with me."

Her voice said 'I'm kidding', but her gaping mouth said otherwise.

I yanked the phone out of her hand, fumbling when she gripped it tighter and we momentarily wrestled it from each other. When I had it safely back in my possession, I smiled at her triumphantly. She rolled her eyes and playfully shook her head.

"Whatever twat, have it... *shit*." Rosie's eyes were cast downward, staring at Ryder's picture, still pulled up on my phone.

"What?!" I asked, looking down on the phone too.

That's when I saw it. The worst possible thing I could have seen in that moment.

A blue thumbs up.

I had liked a picture.

I stared at the little blue thumb under the photo.

No.

No.

NO.

SHIT.

I slammed my head against the back of the couch, closed

my eyes and let my phone fall from my grasp and into my lap. Dammit.

"Well..." Rosie drawled, voice trailing off. My eyes snapped open, my blue eyes locking with her hazel.

"I'm going to kill you." I shot daggers at her through my eyes, but unfortunately, my glare did nothing to frighten her. Clearly my bark was worse than my bite, but really even my bark was more like a dull woof.

"He probably won't even notice, friend. Guys don't pay attention to stuff like that. I'll bet he doesn't even log on."

She barely finished that sentence before my phone pinged, alerting me that I had a new Facebook message. Raising the phone to eye level, my eyes widened as the message automatically pulled up. My phone slipped through my fingers like it had scalded me, and Rosie scooped it up before I had the opportunity to reach back out and grab it.

"Oh my God!" she squealed. "It's from *him*!"

I reached for my phone, but she stood up, walking away as she read the message aloud.

Ryder Thompson: Hey. How are you doing?

Such a simple message, but Rosie outwardly swooned. I groaned, burying my face into the nearest pillow, thankful that my hands landed on chenille rather than the rougher canvas one next to it. At least my face would be cushy when I wallowed in self-pity.

I was mortified.

How did this even happen?

Fingers tapped quickly as Rosie worked to type a response back to Ryder. I launched myself off the couch, lunging at her faster than my brain could compute, in a race to get my phone.

"Oh, no you don't. You've already done enough damage for one night, don't you think?" I said, pinning her with an icy glare while I yanked the phone from her grip. She rolled her eyes at me, huffing, as she crossed her arms across her chest.

"Fine, but you can't just ignore him. You have to respond!"

I locked the screen and pocketed the phone. "I will. Later. Maybe. Do you want to start a movie?"

I fell back down on my couch and kicked my feet up onto the ottoman, reaching for the remote. A distraction to this utter travesty is what I need.

"Nah, I'm gonna head home."

I cocked an eyebrow at her, glancing at my watch. It was barely seven-thirty.

"Boo," I said, giving her a pouty lip. "That's no fun."

She laughed as she walked around my studio and gathered up her belongings. Every time she came over, it was like a Rosie tornado hit—I had even invested in a designated basket, which I placed on a small table by the door, dedicated to just the things she left behind. Because she left something behind, every single time.

She glanced around my small space one more time before padding over to me, her bare feet making light pitter-patters on the tile as she approached.

Leaning down, she planted a wet, lip-glossy kiss on my cheek. "Love you, bitch. Write him back." She tossed me a wink on her way out, letting the door slam behind her. I chuckled to myself as I wiped the sticky gloss off my cheek and went over to my door to lock it behind her.

My best friend was a firecracker, but I loved her dearly for it.

SITTING in the darkness of my studio, the only light that illuminated came from the screen of my phone as I reread the message from Ryder. We were now approaching the two-hour mark of not responding and my subconscious told me that I needed to reply soon, or not at all. I was still within the acceptable window where I could play off my lack of response due to being distracted, but waiting much longer would force me to either not respond at all, or look like I had been severely overthinking this response. Which I was, but he certainly wouldn't need to know that. Although now that I was thinking about my overthinking, I realized there was about a one percent chance he was even thinking about my impending response.

He was, after all, a married man with a child. Surely he wasn't sitting on the other end of his phone staring at the screen like I was. I exhaled, mustering up my courage and typed out a response.

Elle Peters: Hey! It's been forever! I've been good. Busy, but good! How about you?

I clicked send before I chickened out.

My jaw hit the floor as his tiny circular photo popped up next to my message immediately, indicating he had read it. Equally as fast, another message appeared on my screen.

Ryder Thompson: Been good. My son Jordan is eight now. I started a contracting company a while back, so that's been keeping me busy.

No mention of Lily... weird.

Elle Peters: Wow! That's awesome. Still living in Shadow Hills?

I slapped my palm to my forehead. *Why* did I just ask him that?!

Ryder Thompson: Yeah. Still in L.A.?

My heart skipped a beat. *He remembered where I moved to.*

Elle Peters: Nope, actually I moved to Ridgewood a few years ago. It was close enough to coming home without coming home.

Ryder Thompson: Why didn't you want to come home?

My fingers lingered over the touch screen keyboard of my

phone, not sure how to answer. I couldn't tell him that I didn't come home because of him, because I couldn't bear to see his happy family and my heart wouldn't be able to heal from that.

No, I couldn't tell him that, obviously.

But what could I say?

What lie was good enough to let fall from my lips that also harbored some semblance of the truth? Because the entire reason that I avoid Shadow Hills is because I need to continue avoiding him. It had been eight years, but I was wholly confident that if I saw him, my entire being would crumble.

And if I saw him with his family?

I would turn to dust and simply cease to exist.

So what could I say? How could I respond to him without spewing the bitter truth: that Shadow Hills was the place I avoided because running into him would be salt in the wound that still hadn't fully healed after eight years.

Elle Peters: Because it wasn't home anymore.

Ha. Good answer, Elle.

Grinning triumphantly, I mentally patted myself on the back. My smile instantly fell though, when I read the response that came through just as quickly as I had sent mine.

Ryder Thompson: I get that. It's felt like something was missing for a long time now.

I stared at my phone, rereading his message thirty times before I finally sat the phone down next to me on the couch.

The overthinking was happening again, and I analyzed every single potential meaning within that message.

What's been missing? Did he mean me? Did he miss me? Had something else happened in Shadow Hills that I hadn't been aware of? I had asked my parents not to tell me anything about *anything*, so maybe I missed *something*. Were he and Lily still married? He hadn't said anything about her, but did mention their son.

My head fell back onto the couch cushion and I closed my

eyes, focusing on my breathing to slow my racing heart. At the end of the day, Ryder was a boy. No, correction, we were in our late 20s now. Ryder was a man. But the thing about men is that they never say what they mean, at least in my experience with them, and whatever they do say is usually a lot more simple than my female brain transforms it into.

Somehow, in my spiral of overthinking, I began to mentally reminisce about my past relationships since I left Shadow Hills. There hadn't been that many, but enough where I had picked up a thing or two and really honed in on what I wanted out of a relationship and in a man.

I had dated some real losers, all the relationships never getting past the four-month mark because of one of their various screwups, but I also knew that I wasn't innocent when it came to screwing it up in my own way, too.

"Emotionally unavailable" is what the last boyfriend, Gage, had called me.

Gage was a looker with his light brown, perfectly styled hair and dark brown eyes. If I was being perfectly honest, his physique didn't hurt, either. What good ol' Gage was lacking, however, was any sort of compassion, empathy, or overall human decency. He was the jerk who snapped his fingers at waitstaff to get their attention, let the door slam in little old ladies' faces while walking into a building, and the one who always sent his mother to voicemail.

The only reason why I stuck around for so long—if you count six weeks as long—was because the sex was good. He knew how to take care of his women in bed, which was the extent of his taking care of abilities. When I eventually broke it off with him, the final straw being when he left a $5 tip on a $125 meal, he was less than pleased. I didn't have the chance to explain why I was no longer interested because he called me "an emotionally unavailable bitch" before he reached over me to open my car door, signaling for me to get out.

The memory still makes me laugh.

Since my lovely time with Gage, I had been blissfully single, but now as I sat here with my head against the couch and the lingering sensation to pick up the phone and continue my message chat with Ryder, I contemplated if I really was emotionally unavailable.

I had built my walls up, brick by brick, and no one had truly ever crashed them down. I hadn't let them, but I also hadn't wanted anyone to.

Later that night, while in bed, I stared at Ryder's last message to me and debated heavily about responding or just letting it go. It had been a one off that we had even exchanged a few messages, and he hadn't reached out again after I stopped responding to him. Why would he? He was probably lying in bed right now, next to Lily, talking about their day or making love.

I groaned, tossing my arm over my eyes. Why did I have to let my mind go there?

Because that's what people in relationships do, dummy. That's what married people do.

Ugh. I was growing more frustrated by the second. This is exactly why I had avoided anything to do with him. This feeling right here. I let myself stew inside for another twenty minutes or so before I reached over and plugged in my phone, then tossed it on the floor.

Rosie owed me a stiff drink after tonight.

CHAPTER ELEVEN

Elle

Two weeks had gone by since message-gate and I was anxious to finish work for the day. Working my way up at *The Daily Reader* hadn't been a simple task, being that it was a small newspaper with a team of around twenty, but I had managed to become one of their main writers and I was damn proud of myself for that. I had been putting in long hours and all the extra stress had paid off when I received my promotion last year.

Today had been a tough day creatively for me. My mind wasn't in it. I was tired, and more than ready for the weekend —which was still a couple of days away. I had just forced myself to refocus rather than just zoning out to music when my email pinged. I glanced at the clock before navigating the mouse over to my email account. My lips pursed in confusion when my inbox reflected no unread messages.

Had I imagined it?

My eyes narrowed, skimming the screen before realizing that my personal email was pulled up in a secondary tab. I clicked over to bring up my personal email and saw the unread message. A gasp fell from my lips when I saw who the message was from, and excitement bloomed in my chest

Sender: NoWhit20@mailee.com
Subject: A Million Years Later
Hey Elle,

Wow, it's been a long time! I heard you were back in town. I know it's a little out of the blue for me to send this email, but I had hoped you would reach out to me once you were settled. That doesn't seem to be the case since I heard you came back a few years ago, so I wanted to reach out to you and see how you were. I would love to meet up with you and catch up. Could we go for a drink this weekend? Friday? Reggie's, 7PM?

Let me know your plans. I would love to see you.

I miss you, Elle.

-Noah

A smile crept across my face as I reread the email twice more. It had been a long time since I had seen or talked to Noah and I really did want to catch up with him, but my mind was struggling to process that I had heard from both Ryder and now Noah in the span of just a couple of weeks.

Why now?

And why so close together?

Was it purely coincidence, or were they friends now and had spoken about me? That wouldn't have been the most off the wall thing considering at one point Noah and Lily had been... uh, friends?

I shook off that possibility, remembering the odd tension in the air when I overheard Noah and Lily's spat. That was sexual tension, I was sure of it, so the chances of a friendship between Ryder and Noah, especially one where they sat around discussing me, was unlikely. It had to just be coincidence, but I couldn't stop myself from overthinking yet again.

Losing my friendship with Noah after I left Shadow Hills was something that took me a long time to move past. I hadn't reached out to him since moving back because I know that I had handled things poorly when I left town—I had been immature and selfish. He had been my best friend and rock throughout my entire childhood and teenage years, but something about me moving so suddenly after graduation had him acting strangely toward me and frankly, the bitterness was ugly on him. So I made the rash decision to leave without saying goodbye, heated in the argument we had two days before I left.

Could I have handled it better?

Uh, yeah.

Did I though?

Nope.

Noah had begged me to stay a few more weeks into summer, but I refused; the night of graduation was a painful memory I was desperate to flee. He had called me selfish and said some other choice words about my decision, so in a rush of teenage hormones I acted irrationally, giving him a giant middle finger by leaving without so much as a goodbye.

To say that strained our friendship would be an understatement. I could now count how many times we had spoken since on one hand. Spoiler alert, it was a big fat zero.

For years, it had felt like a giant piece of me was missing, but I just couldn't bring myself to rebuild the bridge after I moved back. Instead, I forced myself to constantly look forward. I had to in order to survive the fallout. Never look back, always forward.

Truthfully, after I moved back, I was just too nervous to reach out despite how many times I wanted to. I drafted email after email, and dialed his old phone number so many times, but never had the guts to push send or connect the call. The Elle I had been the last few weeks before I left was not the Elle that I am today, and whenever I thought of Noah, I found it difficult to separate the two Elles, so I slapped a Band-Aid over the festering wound that was our not-so-forgotten friendship and pushed forward.

With my fingers hovering over the keyboard, I thought purposefully about what I wanted to say back to Noah. There were so many words left unspoken that I felt like I needed to carefully craft this email. My heart was pounding so rapidly in my chest that my head started to feel floaty and my palms started sweating *again*.

I let out a shaky breath as I reread the email a few times, that agreed to drinks, before finally hitting send. It was short, but to the point. We would have to hash everything out on Friday night, and I realized in that moment how much I hoped that the fragments of our old friendship would still be visible when we saw each other again. Noah was a piece of the puzzle that had been missing and I hadn't realized until now how desperate I was to have his friendship back.

Knowing that there was zero chance of refocusing on my work for the day, I slammed my laptop shut and started cleaning up my desk so that I could head home.

I let my mind wander back to the memory of graduation night as I made my way to my car. It was the first time in a long time I let the thoughts of Ryder from that night invade my head, and sadness pulled at my heart. The sadness quickly dissipated as anger overtook, burning fiercely within me for allowing myself to *still* pine over a guy who I had never even kissed. A guy who I had not only never kissed, but a guy who had a wife and a child—maybe even a couple of children by this point. He was never even mine to begin with, yet the feelings were still buried within me.

Stupid, stupid Elle. *This* is why I forced myself to build

mental walls against *myself*, because sometimes the 'what-if' hurt so bad I found it hard to breathe. I was a fool, but I also wasn't that girl anymore. I had grown from being the girl who would allow herself to be pulled into the darkness of her thoughts and stomp on her own self-confidence.

Too much time had passed, and I had grown too much.

I worked so hard to become the person who I am right here, right now. I have flourished in my career, achieved goals I was told I would never achieve. I had dated, and although the relationships always had a short expiration date, I *had* realized that they just weren't living up to the expectations that I had built in my head.

That was growth, right?

I knew that my ridiculous expectations were just a means of staying closed off and guarded, and I knew that I needed to pull myself out of the slump and get back out there. It was just always such a hard admission to make.

Maybe meeting up with Noah would be just the kick start that I needed to start really living again.

As I drove home, I called Rosie just to hear her voice, and found myself asking her if she wanted to grab a drink later. She owed me one, and it had been a few months since I had been at Reggie's. It made sense to stop in a few days ahead of mine and Noah's meet up. Maybe the familiarity would calm my nerves that I knew would be insane come Friday.

AROUND 8 O'CLOCK MY phone chimed, letting me know my Uber was out front waiting for me. I hurried to grab my purse and keys, locking up behind me as I followed the dimly lit path to the driveway and climbed into the dark sedan waiting for me. The Uber driver was a small, redheaded woman who looked to be in her mid to late forties. We exchanged pleasantries for the fifteen-minute drive and I thanked her as I climbed out of her car, offering a small wave after the door had shut.

Rosie sat on the top part of a bench outside of the bar, waiting for me with a cigarette dangling from her fingers.

"You're still smoking? I thought you quit." I wrinkled my nose, watching as she tossed it to the floor and used the platform of her heel to snuff it out on the ground.

"You win some, you lose some." She shrugged, looping her arm through mine.

Once inside, we found a couple of barstools and ordered two drinks; a rum and Coke for me and a whisky neat for her.

"Brent broke up with me, again."

I tried to hide my eye roll, taking a sip of my drink while trying to formulate a response that would make me sound like less of a bitch and more of a good friend. "I'm so sorry, Rosie, but maybe it's for the best? You guys have been so on and off since the beginning. What if he's your Scott Disick and by finally leaving him, you'll get to meet your Travis Barker? Well, assuming they end up being endgame."

She pursed her lips, contemplating my words as she stared into her drink. I mentally thanked TikTok for giving me that inspirational tidbit, as it seemed to do exactly what I had hoped and was pushing Rosie into a better mood. She smiled at me and polished off her drink, quickly hopping down from her barstool before pulling me off of mine, nearly knocking me over in the process. I glared at her, but her smile was infectious. Letting her pull me out onto the bar's small dance floor, I bobbed awkwardly beside her before finally letting go, allowing the music to flow through my body. With a drink in one hand and the other up in the air, I moved my hips to the beat, swaying and letting the confidence bubble within me. It wasn't long before we had the eyes of nearly every guy glued to us as we moved our hips and grinded on each other.

After several songs of nonstop dancing, I gestured to Rosie that we should move back to the bar for a break. Nodding her head once, she grabbed my hand as I led us back to the same barstools we had occupied earlier. I situated myself before turning my body toward the bar, scanning the length of it in search of the bartender. My eye caught on a guy sitting at the opposite end of the bar chatting animatedly with his friend, and I licked my lips as his eyes instantly locked with mine. He was hot as sin and, while clearly still in mid-sentence; he undressed me with his eyes. Suppressing a grin, the bartender appeared in front of me and I turned my attention to him, ordering iced water for both me and Rosie.

She groaned at my order choices. "Water?! Bitch, the night is still young and we have a lot more dancing to do."

"Don't worry, we're not done dancing yet. I'm just done with drinking for the night," I told her, laughing as she wrinkled her nose.

"That's a shame. I was just about to ask if I could buy you a drink," a gruff voice spoke from behind me. I swiveled on my barstool to find the handsome guy from across the bar now standing next to me.

"I work tomorrow morning, but thanks." Looking up at him from below my lashes, I shrugged nonchalantly.

"How about a dance, then?"

I gained a newfound confidence as I slid from my barstool, kissing Rosie on the cheek before walking ahead of bar guy slowly, hips sashaying as I moved.

"You coming?" I asked from over my shoulder.

With a pep in his step, he followed me to the dance floor.

As if the universe was trying to be a complete cliche, the next song on the bar's playlist had a slower beat, giving bar guy time to talk while he pulled me into an embrace. "River" by Bishop Briggs, which if you've ever heard is the epitome of sex, blasted through the sound system, forcing us to move slowly and sensually.

Seeming to be caught in the low tones of the song, bar guy spoke, his voice husky. "I'm Matt."

Of course, this guy's name was Matt.

Matt is the guy you can bring home to mom and dad, the nice, safe, practical choice in life. Guys named Matt inevitably end up being dull.

"Elle," I told him, choosing to close the gap between us to see if the feeling of his body against mine would invoke a spark of chemistry. His hands slid down my back, stopping just barely above my ass, as he continued to sway me.

As the song changed to a fast one, thank God, we broke apart and upped our pace, letting the music take over our bodies and guide us in the movements. It surprised me when I realized at least an hour had passed.

I turned to him and yelled over the music, "I need to find my friend!"

Not waiting for a response, I walked toward the bar, looking for Rosie over the sea of people who filled in every gap. My pulse quickened when I couldn't find her. I forced myself to not panic and pulled out my phone. There was a text waiting for me from thirty minutes ago.

Rosie: FOUND BRENT'S REBOUND, TXT ME TOMRW. LOVEEEEEEE YOU BITCHHHH.

I would like to say that I was surprised she had left, but this was classic Rosie behavior and one of the reasons why I preferred when we hung out anywhere other than a bar or club. Inevitably, if she was single, I got left in the dust at some point for a random bar hook up. Still staring down at my phone, I made a split decision to grab life by the balls and get out of my comfort zone. Take a page out of Rosie's playbook.

I had been thinking about Ryder all day, which was ridiculous, considering I hadn't seen him in, how many years now?

But after scrolling through his Facebook photos and replacing my memory of Ryder with an absolutely gorgeous, completely ripped *adult* Ryder, he had been creeping into my every thought.

Not to mention I was growing increasingly nervous to meet up with Noah in just two days. The only time that I wasn't thinking about *anything* was when I was dancing with what's his face. And if that wasn't a sign, I wasn't sure what was.

"Do you want to get out of here?" I asked bar guy, my heart pounding wildly in my chest. I had never asked a guy that I had just met to go home with me. Never. It just wasn't my thing. I was now navigating uncharted waters.

He smiled, nodding his head eagerly. "My place or yours?" he asked.

"Yours."

Shit. Let's hope that I wasn't about to go home with a serial killer.

CHAPTER TWELVE

Elle

Going home with the guy from the bar probably wasn't the best idea I've ever had. After letting Ryder invade my thoughts after so many months of *not* thinking of him, I needed to at least try to finish out the night without him on my mind. Much to my dismay, my efforts were completely wasted. There was just no escaping the thought of him. I knew that spending the night with a hot guy wouldn't rid him from my thoughts, but here I was, giving it a shot anyway.

I thought about backing out—making some excuse and hightailing it out of here. I could say no and leave as quickly as I said yes, but as the guy from the bar fumbled with the zipper of my jeans, I realized not only did I not want to go through with this; I *needed* to.

Ryder was very much still married and I—I had unfortunately realized that I was still infatuated with him.

Eight. Fucking. Years. Later.

Bar guy and I undressed quickly, our kisses frantic, sloppy, and full of teeth. He lightly pushed me down on the bed, watching as my boobs bounced on impact. A hungry growl escaped him as his eyes hooded with desire.

I, on the other hand, felt nothing.

He moved down my body, licking and nipping as he traveled south, and I watched him with boredom. I stopped him just as he reached my center, pulling him back up and meeting his lips in a bruising kiss. Reaching between us, I caressed his length, hard and ready to go.

"Do you have a condom?" I asked, peeking up at him beneath my lashes. I was playing coy, trying to come off as interested in this as he was.

The bed dipped as he leaned over and reached for his pants off the floor, pulling a condom from his pocket. I choked a laugh back down my throat as he tore the wrapper with his teeth; a move I had only seen done in movies and wasn't nearly as sexy as it would have been on the big screen. He rolled the condom down his shaft, pumping it a few times, watching as I laid back and made myself comfortable beneath him. He used his fingers to play at my entrance for a moment, checking to see if I was as ready for him as he was for me. I wasn't, but he felt that I was wet enough for him to go for it. He leaned down, pressing his lips against mine as he thrust into me inch by inch. It had been a while since a man had been inside me, and I let out a hiss as my body adjusted to his.

He stilled, waiting until I gave a slight nod before he started moving. As he moved in and out of me, my eyes squeezed shut, trying to drown out the sounds of his grunts.

Maybe this was a mistake. He was trying to make it pleasurable for me, he really was, but he just kept missing the mark.

Maybe if I kept my eyes closed, I could imagine it was Ryder slipping in and out of me right now instead of what's-his-name from the bar. Suddenly, the fantasy played in front of my eyes like a movie.

Ryder's hand slipping down between my legs, feeling the pulse beating in my most intimate parts and making circular motions in a way he just knew I would like. His breath mingling with mine as he hovered above, lost in pleasure.

My heart rate started to increase, and I felt the vibration of a low moan escape past my lips. Bar guy thought it was for him and sped up his pace, pounding into me more frantically. The realization that I could actually salvage this and get myself to the point of orgasm had me tilting my head to reach his ear.

"Mike, flip me over," I whispered breathily.

"It's Matt," he responded between grunts, and my cheeks burned with embarrassment. It was clear Matt wouldn't let my slip up ruin the mood though and without hesitation he obliged, pulling out and flipping me like I weighed nothing.

Okay, so maybe that was a little hot. He repositioned himself at my entrance and thrust inside me with one fluid motion, matching the pace he was at before. Snaking his hand around my stomach, his fingers found my clit. He began rubbing circular motions, just as I had fantasied, drawing a moan from me.

Ryder's muscular arms held me close as he fucked me from behind, pounding into me with a force that caused the air to escape my lungs with every thrust. His fingers expertly played with that sensitive bud while his other hand grasped my breast roughly, pulling me back into him as we moved at a faster pace. His growls vibrated through me as he circled his hips, biting down on my shoulder while I screamed his name.

Within seconds, I was crying out, shaking as I climaxed hard, my walls throbbing and tightening around Ryder's hardness inside of me.

As I came down from the clouds, though, reality snapped me out of the moment.

This wasn't Ryder holding me close and kissing my neck.

This wasn't Ryder pulling out of me.

As my orgasm subsided, shame began to wash over me, but I refused to let it. I was a single, consenting adult, and I can guarantee I wasn't the only woman tonight, somewhere in this world who had or was having an orgasm while fantasizing about another man.

Repositioning myself on the bed, I looked up at bar guy, watching him roll the soiled condom off of his shaft and dispose it into the trash can by his bed. He positioned himself beside me, laying on his side and propping himself up by his arm so that he could look at me. Both of us were still naked and I could see his eyes rake over my entire body before landing back on my face. The urge to cover myself engulfed me as he licked his bottom lip, his eyes darkening. I could tell he wanted to say something, but I stopped him by leaning forward and pressing a quick kiss against his cheek before he could.

"I've got to go," I told him, rolling away from him and off the bed. I bent down to grab my dress and threw it over my head, searching for my panties. After locating them, I pulled them on and decided to skip the bra, tossing it into my open purse instead. He said nothing, watching in silence, as I sat in the chair beside the bed and pulled my heels back on.

"Can I get your number? I'd love to take you out some-time," he asked, confidence waning as he watched me trying to get out of there as fast as possible.

I wavered, deciding whether to just be cordial and give him my number or to shoot him down completely. I wasn't the type who could lead a guy on and not feel guilty about it, but I had also never been in a one-night stand situation, so I was really unsure of how to handle myself at the moment. I looked down, willing my brain to make a choice and say some-thing, *anything*, because at this point I was making it awkward.

Thankfully, bar guy, ever the gentleman, let me off the hook.

He slipped off the bed so quietly I hadn't even realized he

was standing in front of me until he gently cupped my face with one hand.

"Hey, it's okay, I get it," he said softly, tilting my head to look him in the eyes. We stared at each other for a minute before I burst out laughing, the sweet and tender moment ruined by his dick hanging limp between his legs as he stood there, still completely naked. He let go of my face, laughing as he took a step back, shrugging his shoulders.

Knowing that no other words needed to be said, I pulled on my sweater and secured my purse strap on my shoulder as I reached for the doorknob. I gave bar guy one more awkward glance and a friendly laugh as I stepped out of the threshold and shut the door behind me.

CHAPTER THIRTEEN

Ryder

My heart raced as the feeling of Elle's body slid down mine, my hands grasping her perfect ass until she had moved so far down that I could no longer reach it. I drank in the sight of her hovering above my cock, her ass in the air giving me a view of the sexiest black lace panties, while she licked her lips and started pulling at my briefs. My rock hard cock sprang free from the elastic and she looked up at me from below her lashes, the heat of her breath so close to my skin it gave me goosebumps. She took my cock in her hand, using her finger to trace the vein on the bottom. Opening her mouth, she leaned forward...

I woke with a startle, a layer of sweat coating my body and my cock harder than it had been in years. That was the most vivid dream, and a wave of guilt hit me as I felt Lily's warm body roll over beside me. She snaked her hand across my bare chest, her eyes still closed.

"Are you okay?" she whispered, trailing her fingers across my collarbone, sleep thick in her voice.

"Yeah, it's okay, go back to sleep," I told her, covering my hand over hers and squeezing lightly. She squeezed back and pulled her hand away, readjusting herself on her pillow. Her eyes never opened and within seconds her light breaths told me she was peacefully back asleep. I laid there burning a hole in the ceiling, wondering how my life had gotten to this point.

Years of memories swam through my head; Jordan's birth, our small backyard wedding, starting my contracting business, Lily's constant support, family dinners, watching Jordan grow and flourish, Christmases, birthdays.

I've been happy, I really have, but something's been missing. Something I had buried deep within me and locked down tight. *Someone*, actually. Visions of the doe-eyed brunette that I said goodbye to all those years ago danced before my eyes, sending a stabbing feeling straight through my chest. Elle had been and will always be the one that got away. The sacrifice I made to give my son the life that he deserved. I shut my eyes tightly, letting my mind wander back to our conversation just weeks ago as sleep took me yet again.

The brassy sound of my 5:00 A.M. alarm came all too quickly. I reached over to turn it off, trying to avoid waking Lily this early. She had another hour to rest before she'd need to be up to get Jordan ready for school. It was hard to believe he was already in elementary school. Most days I felt like I was stuck between living in a constant state of fast-forward, while simultaneously living in slow motion. We went through the daily grind, our lives rich with monotony. The years had flown by, but goddamn it felt like some days the clock refused to fucking move. I was stagnant, bored, and only recently had realized what I needed in my life to feel *alive*.

I loved Lily. She's the mother of my child, for Christ's sake, but she had never made my cock as hard as it had been one fantasy and a few hours prior.

Forcing myself out of bed, I made my way to our shared walk-in closet, pulling the door closed behind me before turning on the light. I stood motionless, forcing myself to get a grip. It was just a dream. I needed to forget about it and move on with my day. Remind myself why I chose this life. The end goal was always to give Jordan the life he deserved. I would never become my father.

After going through the motions of dressing, brushing my teeth, and making sure my bedhead wasn't too bad, I grabbed my wallet, keys, and Hydro Flask before heading out the door to my work truck. It had been three years, but pride still bloomed in my chest every time I saw the words *Thompson Contracting* on the side of my truck. Years of working construction had paid off and with the encouragement of my family, I was able to jumpstart my business, and was recently voted "Best Contractor in Shadow Hills". Not bad for a kid who was forced to grow up.

Throughout my workday my thoughts continuously wandered to the dream I had, still mentally cursing myself for reaching out to Elle through messenger a few weeks back. It was a dumb move, but one that I couldn't resist after seeing that she had liked my picture. We weren't friends on any social media and it was obvious that she had looked me up that night.

Had she been thinking about me over the years, like I had been thinking of her?

It was stupid to think of her at all; I had closed the door on any sort of possibility of her the night of graduation, but I couldn't help myself from time to time. I had never tried to speak with her before now, and our message exchange almost felt like I had crossed a line. But it had been innocent, and it was going to stay innocent. The dream happened because I was horny, plain and simple. I just needed to get laid. By my *wife*.

Lily and I had a mediocre sex life. I was no stranger to dirty dreams, but what had been surprising was seeing Elle's face so vividly. Sex with Lily was satisfying enough, but not so much where after the dream, I felt compelled to wake her to reenact it. With Lily, things felt so... habitual. I liked to think of myself as generous in bed, never finishing until Lily finished first, but we lacked the frenzy. We lacked passion. My wife was beautiful, but we weren't in a hurry to rip each other's clothes off, and there was no spontaneity. I couldn't throw her onto the kitchen counter and fuck her into oblivion. We could never just throw a show on for our kid and sneak off for a quickie in the shower.

Sex had become a pre-scheduled event two or three times a month. I was surprised it wasn't marked on the calendar that hung on the pantry door.

Although I still found my wife attractive and I never strayed in our marriage, I was bored. Fuck, was I bored. Our lives had become so routine that sometimes it was stifling, and I felt like I couldn't breathe. But I accepted it because this was the life that I had chosen. I *chose* to become a family man. I made the commitment to Lily when I was hardly even old enough to know the definition of commitment, but I intended to stick by it. At least while our son was young and my wife was still happy.

And she was happy; Lily was spoiled rotten and happy with our lives. She had stayed home with Jordan until he was old enough to go to kindergarten and since then, she had been working part time at Mrs. Landry's floral shop just a few streets away from our house. Lily had always loved photography, but after Jordan was born, she had discovered her love for decorating, which included floral arrangements. The job was perfect for her and helped take a little of the financial burden off of me, so we were both happy.

Maybe the word happy was a stretch, but we certainly were content. We never talked about the past, our decision to have Jordan, or that we had been forced to grow up early and marry young.

We simply went through the motions of life and did everything that we could to remain content with our situation. Nothing had made me question my decisions until now. Now, the what-ifs were filling my head, pulling me back into the past, and making me question everything that I had spent the last eight plus years building.

CHAPTER FOURTEEN

Elle

Pulling open the door to Reggie's, my eyes quickly scanned the bar as I searched for Noah. My shoulders sagged in disappointment when I didn't immediately see him, and I glanced down at my watch as I crossed the threshold into the bar. I took my time walking towards it before slipping onto an empty barstool. I leaned across the bar to wave down the bartender as I wondered if I had misread the email and gotten the date wrong. That seemed like a me thing.

"Excuse me, miss, but this seat is reserved for my child-hood best friend," a deep voice rumbled, catching me off guard. My head snapped in the direction of the voice and I was consumed with a wide mixture of emotions; excitement, disbelief, and awe. In front of me was a gorgeous man with breathtakingly rich milk chocolate eyes and hair that was perfectly styled. His trim beard hid the boyish features that I had always admired and made him look like a true man. He wore a crisp blue button up that hugged his biceps in a way that instantly had me wishing he was wearing less so I could see the muscles hidden beneath. And his smile... oh, that smile still looked so incredibly Noah-like. I was surprised I hadn't realized immediately that this eye candy was my best friend.

My Noah.

My Noah had grown up.

He threw his head back in a roar of laughter as I continued to stare with what I could only assume was the most dumbstruck look on my face.

"Wow! Noah! I didn't even recognize you! Oh my gosh, come here!" My shock turned to excitement as I pulled him in for a hug. He was so filled out and the hug felt different from what was engrained in my memory, but I certainly wasn't complaining. His powerful arms devoured me, bringing me a sense of comfort that I hadn't felt in a long, long time.

"Wow," I gasped again, pulling back from the hug to get another good look at him. "I can't believe how much you've changed, Noah! I mean dang, you've really filled out!" I squeezed his bicep, my eyes grazing over him as I awarded him with a catcall whistle.

He smirked, rolling his eyes playfully, and I swear I could see a faint blush coating his cheeks from the attention I was giving him.

"You've changed a lot too, Elle. For one, you've ditched my favorite librarian glasses, and your hair looks a lot different." He grabbed a piece, playing with it. "It's longer, I like it."

"So tell me everything! I can't wait to hear about what you've been up to these last few years," I said enthusiastically. This tall drink of water in front of me was my childhood best friend, and I still couldn't believe it.

His eyes met mine briefly before he fidgeted in his seat, staring at the rows of alcohol bottles lined on display behind the bar. His eyes cast down to his arms that he had folded in front of him as he leaned against the bar top. I could feel his tension and instinctually went to reach for him before dropping my hand back into my lap, thinking better of it.

"Before we get into that, let's start with the elephant in the room, Elle. I asked you here after years of hoping you'd reach out to me and you didn't. I know I could have extended the olive branch too, but honestly, Elle, we both know it isn't my apology to give."

My mouth went slack; his words cut deep and the serious look on his face made my stomach dip. The way he went about bypassing the chit chat was both abrasive and authoritative, and it was in that moment I realized that although he was still my Noah, I truly knew nothing about him anymore. It made me feel uneasy, but I also knew that he was right. Hurt was in his voice as he spoke, and he wasn't the one who owed me anything. I owed him an explanation and an apology, and seeing him after all these years, I was ready to grovel for his forgiveness and his friendship, but I was going to tread carefully. Searching his eyes, I worked out which cards to show while I picked at the white polish on my fingernail, about to lay everything in front of him. But he beat me to it.

"Elle, why did you cut me out of your life completely? Why did you just leave and never look back? You never even bothered to try and mend our friendship after you left. I spent weeks hoping you would just send a text and explain, but there was only silence." It was like he had just taken a knife to my heart. Worse, actually. It was like a knife that had been sitting in a fire, then lodged into my chest, and then pulled out only to have saltwater poured into it.

I was right. He was still angry, and I knew he had every right to be. I had cut him out—ran so far and fast after graduation, because I felt like I was barely treading water. In that moment, I was adamant to do anything that I could to get out of Shadow Hills and away from everything that had hurt me.

Sometimes you make rash decisions when you're barely an adult. You make poor choices. We all make mistakes and we all live with regrets. *My* biggest regret was now sitting next to me at a bar and demanding answers.

My options were clear: face this conversation head on or make a run for it, and I had the feeling that if I chose to continue to sweep this under the rug, Noah would never reach out to me again. It would be the final nail in the coffin of our friendship that I had already thought was dead.

Exhaling slowly, I lifted my head up to look him in the eyes. I had thought about what I would say to Noah, if ever given the opportunity, time and time again. This should be easy for me. After all, this was Noah and he would forgive me, right?

He had to forgive me.

As I looked deep into his eyes, we were thirteen again. A core memory hit me like a ton of bricks as I saw it spin through my subconscious like a movie reel.

Me, laying upside down on my bed, my head hanging off the foot of the bed, I watch my door swing open while the blood rushes to my head. Noah stomps into my room, already in a fit of laughter as he aims a Nerf gun right at my forehead and shoots it. The rubber end of the foam bullet bounces off me and lands on the ground, and I somersault off the back of the bed and land at his feet. He's laughing so hard I can see a single tear escape out of the side of his right eye, and I use his blurred vision as the perfect opportunity to swing my legs and sweep him off his feet. Our laughter floats throughout the room and happiness surrounds us.

My eyes are still closed, but I can feel the corners of my mouth turned up as the nostalgic feeling floods my body like a warm embrace. I take my time opening my eyes and when I do, Noah is staring at me intently, watching me with a stoic look. He's always been so patient, loyal, and kind. The impact of my actions from eight years ago hits me like a ton of bricks, and a tear falls. I wipe it away quickly, blinking back the others that threaten to spill.

"I'm so, so sorry, Noah. Let me just preface this entire conversation by starting with this—cutting our communication has always been the biggest regret of my life, and you didn't deserve it. I'm so sorry." I inhaled, letting my next words flow freely so that they're out before I can overthink them. "The night of graduation after you went inside of the house, I stayed sitting by the fire across from Ryder."

He opened his mouth to speak, but I lifted my hand, indicating that I needed to get this out.

"I know you know how I felt about him Noah, and I know that we had a lot of unspoken words back then, about everything surrounding you, me, my feelings for Ryder, and your feelings for Lily. So much happened so quickly and so much was left unsaid. After you went into the house, Ryder opened up to me. He admitted that he was into me but then told me that any possibility of there ever being a him and me, would never happen because he was going to do what was best for his unborn child and for Lily. His mind was already made up. He was going to be the man that his father never was, and that was that. It crushed me, Noah, and it was in that moment that I knew I couldn't stay another minute in Shadow Hills. Between everything going on at home with my parents' divorce, then my mom's crazy coping mechanisms, and finally everything with Ryder, I just couldn't. I couldn't breathe, I couldn't think, I just... I just couldn't anymore." I choked back a sob, looking at him as I continued. "I wasn't strong enough to watch Lily's belly grow any more than it had, and to see their baby after it was born, watch their happiness, their *family* grow and thrive. There was no way my heart could survive that, too. Not when everything else was so broken. I was self-ish, but I was also self-preserving. So I left. I moved up my timeline and got the hell out of there."

Noah looked at me, processing my words.

"But that doesn't explain why you cut me out, Elle. I would

have been there for you. I could have helped you through it. I was going through it too, Elle. So I just don't understand why our friendship had to end just because your high school crush told you he could never be with you."

There was condensation on the side of my glass, and I played with the beads of water. "I don't know. I honestly thought that if I wanted to avoid Shadow Hills, I needed to avoid *all* of Shadow Hills. That included you. You had always been an extension of Shadow Hills. The essence of my entire childhood. It felt easier to just rip the Band-Aid off all at once. I didn't even come home to visit my family for a few years."

"I know," he said, "our moms are best friends, remember?"

I offered a weak smile, now playing with the corner of the soggy napkin underneath my glass. "I'm sorry, Noah."

He didn't accept my apology. There was no "it's okay" or an "I understand." Instead, he said nothing, and I could see his chest rising and falling out of the corner of my eye. I kept my mouth closed, letting him reflect on the explanation that I had given him.

After a long stretch of silence, he spoke, and my heart blossomed with relief. "I went into the police academy about three months after you left."

A smile stretched across my face as he continued. "I've worked my way up over these last couple of years and I'm now up for detective. I'll find out in a couple of weeks if I'll be getting the promotion. Bought a one-bedroom condo here in Ridgewood, which is also where I work, by the way. Ridgewood P.D. I visit my parents once a week on Sundays for dinner—they're still together, still madly in love. I got a dog, Wexley. He's a boxer."

Noah stopped talking suddenly, looking up at me. "You asked me to tell you everything." Grinning at me with his Noah-smirk, he continued to fill me in.

"For a few weeks after you left, I honestly felt like the walls had caved in. I was so mad at you. At the world, really. Bitter at everyone and everything. I started getting into trouble. Fist-fights, mostly. It got to the point where my parents sat me down and gave me an ultimatum. Either I enlisted in some branch of the military or went to a trade school, or I was out of their house for good. So, I figured the police academy was a decent option for me and I applied. They took me and I never looked back."

So many emotions ran through me at once. Surprise over all that he had just shared. Sadness over the emotional turmoil that I had caused him, eventually leading to the ultimatum his parents had given him. Pride over the fact that, despite every-thing, he was living a great, successful life. He even had a dog! I was so happy for him in all that he had accomplished, but I felt like a fool for ever letting my selfishness get in the way of our friendship. Many years had passed us by, and that was entirely my fault.

"What about you, Elle? What have you been up to?"

"Wait a second," I gasped, realizing within Noah's life update he bypassed a crucial detail. "What happened to San Francisco? You were accepted early admission. What happened to leaving for college?"

Noah picked at a string on the cuff of his shirt, his gaze concentrated on the loose threading. "Nothing seemed impor-tant anymore, so I withdrew."

Despair and regret washed through me. "Noah, I'm so incredibly sorry. I know there's nothing that I can say in this moment that will make you believe my regret, but I truly am sorry for how I left things between us and for never trying to mend what I broke. I'm not asking for your forgiveness right now, but I would really love for the chance to prove to you that your friendship has always meant something to me. That *you've* always meant something to me." He gazed at me, reaching over to pull my hand into his. Lacing our fingers together, I could feel the calluses on his palm and the warmth of his hand against mine sent tingles through my body. For the first time in a long time, I felt a sense of peace.

"Yeah, I'd like that Elle, but I need you to promise me one thing."

"Anything," I breathed, and I meant it. All I wanted was my Noah back in my life.

"Next time things get hard, I'm going to need you to talk it out with me. No more running."

"No more running," I promised.

ONCE WE WERE FINISHED REHASHING the past, the rest of our time at the bar was fun and carefree. We had rid ourselves of the heavy topics at the beginning and spent the next few hours sharing everything we could about the last eight years with each other.

Drunk off of each other's company, we lost track of time and realized we had stayed past closing once the bartender gave us the "you don't have to go home but you can't stay here" kick-out line.

Standing to pull my coat on, Noah reached out to help me, turning me slightly while I eased my arms in. His hand brushed lightly along my neck as he released my hair from the back of the jacket and goosebumps pebbled my skin with the lightness of his touch. The sensation was disarming and unexpected, and I began to wonder if there was something about Noah that I hadn't seen until now.

CHAPTER FIFTEEN

Elle

There was something, in fact, that I hadn't seen before and that *something* was the charm that Noah exuded when he was genuinely happy. As children, we were pretty happy most of the time, but the happiness of adult Noah was far more exhilarating than that of young Noah. Adult Noah was constantly up for adventure, and I was having the time of my life as we rebuilt our friendship from the ground up.

Between weeknight dinners and exploring the surrounding cities on the weekends, we saw each other anytime we weren't at work. Some days we'd keep it simple—picnics at the park where we'd lie around for hours with the grass between our toes, or miniature golfing on Friday nights where we'd get stuck behind all the teenagers on their dates. Those were my favorite, actually. Noah and I would narrate our version of what they were saying and try to pick out which bored parent on the sidelines was there to chaperone. Sometimes we'd eat street tacos way too late at night before walking through downtown Ridgewood, window shopping all of the closed storefronts. Other times, though, Noah craved an adrenaline rush. I can't say I always loved this side of our adventures, but

I always gritted my teeth and went along for the ride. Both in the figurative sense and literal. One night, we raced his unmarked squad car. I'm pretty sure *we* could have gotten arrested for that. Where I drew the line was when Noah wanted us to go skydiving. I told him I would watch from the ground and hold a sign that read "I'm free, free falling." He roared a laugh at that one, but never made himself the appointment to go.

Reconnecting with Noah meant also reconnecting with Noah's family, and I was instantly swooped back into their family as though I had never left. I also gave myself the title of stepmom thanks to Wexley, Noah's boxer. We quickly became best friends, and I loved to tease Noah over the fact that if he and I ever stopped talking again, Wexley would rather live with me. We play-fought over our custody agreement frequently.

Before we had realized what had happened, seven months flew by us as if our lives were suddenly in a state of fast forward, the days passing by in a content blur. Being in Noah's presence required zero effort, and I felt genuinely happy again.

One night, while eating Chinese food at his place, Noah stopped talking and suddenly fell deep in thought. He didn't do it often, but it was a telltale Noah sign that he was about to say something he wasn't sure about. Whether it was good news or bad would be reflective on how he started off his sentence, so I held my breath as I waited.

"Do you remember my brother's wedding? When we were eleven?"

That was so long ago, but I guess I could remember bits and pieces of it. I remember I was in it as the flower girl, and that I hated my dress.

"Yeah, I remember. Pretty ironic that I was the one taking you to jail back then, eh, Detective?" I snorted, remembering how much I loved to pretend to be a police officer and take him to jail as a kid. Forget the dolls and dress up, I only wanted to play cops and robbers with Noah.

He rubbed his hand along his chin, at war with himself. He licked his lips before proceeding. His voice was practically a whisper when he asked me, "Do you remember our pact?"

"Why?" I dabbed the corner of my mouth with a napkin before setting it down on the table.

"Do you remember what the pact said?" he asked, his tone serious.

"Yeah...we said that if we weren't married by the time we were 26, we'd marry each other." Sucking in a sharp breath, I realized that we are 26 right now. I was about to be 27. I looked at him with wide eyes, feeling a cool tingle run from my chest down to my toes.

Crap.

Noah reached his hand out quickly to mine and rubbed his fingers over my knuckles. He met my eyes and laughed loudly, seeing the panic all over my face.

"Relax Elle, I am not proposing. Well, I'm not proposing marriage. I think we should see if our relationship could be more than just a friendship, though. Our shit track record began in high school, and clearly we haven't leveled up since." He rubbed his hand over his face. "Look, I know we both have our baggage. There are skeletons that even you don't know about, but you've always helped keep me grounded—even when you weren't in my life. Why not see if we can be a little light in each other's darkness?"

I eyed him with skepticism, wondering if I wanted to cross that line with him. We were practically dating anyway... could there be something else there? I hadn't felt the rush of passion with Noah, but he was comfortable. Fun. He felt like home. And that had to count for something, right?

Wordlessly, I nodded in agreement at everything he was saying.

"Want to see if we have the chemistry to back this?" He gestured between us.

"Okay."

"Yeah?"

"Yeah, I think we should."

He stood, pulling me up with the hand he was still holding, and pressed me tightly against his body. His fingertips grazed my cheek as he tucked a lock of hair behind my ear, his closeness sending a rush through me as he commanded my attention.

"Can I kiss you?"

"I would be disappointed if you didn't," I told him. "We need to test out this chemistry theory."

Wasting no time, his large palm fisted my hair, tilting my head back as his lips met mine. The kiss started slow and sweet, a world of difference from our very first kiss when we were young. Craving more, I deepened the kiss and his tongue quickly found mine. Noah's mouth explored, his tongue caressing mine, and his lips felt pillowy against mine.

He was a great kisser, and while I think we both knew the fireworks weren't exploding instantly, I could still feel the tingling sensation of little butterflies as my body melted into his. A light moan escaped my lips and Noah started moving me backward, guiding me to his couch before he spun our bodies and sat down, my body following his so that I was straddling him.

We spent a long time kissing, touching, and exploring before Noah eventually led me to his bedroom and made love to me for the first time.

Everything about that moment was sweet.

Noah had been sweet.

Sweet had been just what I needed in my life. And I think he needed it too.

CHAPTER SIXTEEN

Elle

Pub 1902 was one of the most popular places to eat for the residents who lived between Shadow Hills and Ridgewood because not only was it a fun, friendly atmosphere, but it was conveniently located almost exactly right on the city limits line. I had been there a few times with Rosie, but it wasn't a place that I liked to frequent because of its proximity to Shadow Hills. We were rapidly approaching ten years, a freaking decade, and I still hadn't run into *him*. It felt like an invisible beacon was keeping me away, but tonight Noah had begged to go somewhere for dinner where we could just hang out, have a beer (him, not me, because ew) and maybe "catch the game on a big screen".

We had been together for several months at this point, having easily fallen into a daily routine by each other's side. Our relationship was the definition of settling, and I was realizing that my love for him was platonic and had been this entire time. Noah was my best friend. He always had been and always will be. He is going to be a fantastic husband and father one day, but frankly, I am relieved every single day that he doesn't propose. Which is completely *not* something someone should think about their boyfriend. Deep down, Noah has to know that this isn't genuine love and that we're both just acting as placeholders for each other.

Platonic placeholders.

Maybe I should get tee-shirts made.

So, here we were pulling into a parking spot outside of the pub, about to have what I hoped would be a quiet, relaxing dinner together. I sent up one last silent prayer that it would be an uneventful night without bumping into anyone that we knew from our present, or otherwise. Our ten-year high school reunion was next weekend, and I had enough anxiety over that. All I wanted was one more weekend of normalcy before our past bubbled up and became our present.

I stepped out of the car, clutching my Kindle and situating my purse on my shoulder before glancing around the parking lot. The air felt wet, crisp, and cool after the rain cleared up a few hours ago. Noah came around from the driver's side and took my hand, lacing his warm fingers through mine. I smiled at him; though his touch didn't send shivers down my spine or make the butterflies in my stomach go crazy, he still felt like home. He felt safe, happy, and familiar. We had achieved a lot together over the last several months, and our relationship fell into a very tranquil spot, but I struggled daily with the feeling that I was letting both Noah and myself down.

Our hands broke apart when the waitress showed us to our table and handed us a menu. Staring down at us from the edge of the table, she smacked loudly on a piece of gum as she took our drink order. Noah ordered for me, knowing that I never strayed from my girly drinks.

"Dos Equis for me, and she'll have a margarita on the rocks, strawberry."

The waitress' bubble popped. "Salt or sugar on the rim, sweetheart?" she asked, turning her attention to me.

Our waitress was really pretty with soft brown eyes, her

lips painted with a light pink lipstick. Her light brown hair was in a high ponytail and she had a small nose ring on the right side of her nose. She had a floral sleeve tattooed on her left arm, and I couldn't help but wish that I had the guts to do something like that. I could never pull off a sleeve of tattoos, though.

Realizing that I was staring and taking too long to respond, I hastily told her salt when I should have said sugar.

Who gets salt on a strawberry margarita? I guess there's a first time for everything and I just hoped that it wasn't going to be weird and gross. Worst-case scenario, I could brush it off with a napkin. I could feel my brows furrow and knew that I had done it again; I was lost inside of my own head. My anxiety creeped up, and I wondered if I had drawn an audience. I looked up at Noah and found him watching me. *Of course.*

"Can we switch sides so I can see the game?" he asked, already sliding out of his chair. *I guess he didn't notice my weirdness.*

"Sure," I muttered as I stood, pushing my chair back and grabbing my purse from the side of the chair. He reached for my hand and gave it a squeeze as we switched sides, and as I sat down again, I pulled my Kindle out of my purse. If he was going to get lost in the football game, I was absolutely going to get lost in the new R.J. Lewis book that I had just downloaded.

Aside from being *platonic placeholders* for each other, we had totally become that couple—the ones who don't even talk when they're at restaurants because they're so comfortable with each other that there is literally nothing new to talk about. I wasn't sure if that was a boring relationship or a secure one. My guess wasn't the latter, especially since I could map out how the rest of our night would go.

We'd order our food, eat in silence, Noah's eyes glued to

the TV, mine glued to my Kindle. As his heart was racing about the potential touchdown, mine would be racing about the hot male character in my book that was about to touch the heroine for the first time. Noah would pay for dinner, we'd go back to his place, or mine, and I'd suggest we reenact what I had just read in my book.

This would get Noah all hot and bothered (he definitely didn't mind when I read spicy books). He'd end up wanting to take a shower first, then after his shower, one of two things would happen. Either Noah would initiate the sex I had suggested earlier, or he would tell me he was too tired and that he had to work early the next morning. If we had sex, I'd stay the night, but if we didn't, I'd feign a yawn and head home. Either way, I knew I would be going to sleep with an orgasm, whether it was courtesy of Noah or my bright pink bestie in the drawer of my bedside table.

It's official. I'm getting the tee-shirts made.

CHAPTER SEVENTEEN

Ryder

Holy shit. Holy fucking shit.

My hand was frozen on the handle of the door to Pub 1902.

It had been almost 10 years since I had seen her, but there was no doubt in my mind that the stunning woman sitting toward the back of the restaurant was Elle.

I stared through the door like a fucking creeper until an elderly woman approached, giving me a pointed look as she eagerly waited for me to open the door. I was a little too rough as I opened it and waited for the woman to walk through. Stepping in after her, I rushed to the hostess stand and turned my back toward the restaurant to shield my face. I stood there lost in thought before my mind came back into focus when the woman behind the podium popped her gum loudly. Meghan, her name tag, read. I told her I was there to pick up food under the name of Lily, and she walked away to go get my order.

Did I dare turn around? She was so close, and who was she here with? Questions raced through my mind, flashbacks of young Elle looking at me over the flames of a fire on the last night I saw her. I turned my body slightly, putting her table in my line of sight. She was looking down at some sort of tablet and a small smile pulled at her lips as her eyes skimmed over whatever she was looking at. The man she was with had his back to me and I couldn't make out who it was, but I felt a powerful sensation burn through me with every fiber of my being. *Jealousy.* It was a feeling I had lost touch with, an emotion that I had long since felt. Nothing throughout my entire ten-year marriage with Lily had ever made me jealous, yet here I was standing in a restaurant staring at a girl, *a woman*, that I had zero right to have any emotions for, spewing with jealousy. I watched her sit up straighter and set her device down on the table. Just as she began shifting in her seat, I twisted my body back around, not wanting to be caught staring at her. This was not the time or the place for a trip down memory lane.

As soon as the waitress returned and handed me my food, I wasted no time getting the fuck out of there, nearly ripping the door off its hinges as I bolted.

THAT NIGHT, after returning home with our food, Lily, Jordan, and I ate in silence. When Jordan was finished devouring his plate, he asked to be excused, cleared his dish, and headed back up to his room to turn his video game back on. I waited silently until I heard him speaking with a friend through his mic. When his headphones are on is when Lily and I choose to have the conversations we don't want him overhearing. I knew he wouldn't hear us now, so it was time for us to have a conversation about our marriage.

I knew what was missing in my life within that three-minute span at the pub. I think I always knew, I was just never brave enough to admit it to myself. We had always been open and honest with each other, and I wasn't about to start lying to her now. She needed to know that I saw Elle, and she needed to know that it fucked me up in the head.

I broke the silence, my heart beating wildly in my chest. "Lily...." I started, but she cut me off.

"Ry, I need to talk to you."

Fuck. The last time she started a sentence like that was eleven years ago, and she was pregnant with Jordan. I swear my heart stopped beating. I could feel the beads of sweat at my hairline and my palms went clammy.

We said no more kids. We had agreed years ago that we were done. Fuck.

Our eyes met from across the table and I could see the tears in her eyes welling up. All the air squeezed from my lungs.

"I'm not happy," she blurted. "I'm bored. God, I'm so fucking bored, Ryder. We've become this old married couple who doesn't do shit and barely has a sex life and is just *boring*. I hate it. How did we get here?" A tear fell from her eye and I watched it stream down her cheek and land in her lap. She wiped the second tear before it made it that far.

I mulled over her words.

We got here because we married out of obligation, not love.

That was the truth. The hard, cold reality of our lives and the reason we had both wasted the last ten years. I raked my teeth over my bottom lip, staring at her as she stared at me. "Lily..." I began again, the scenario I had thought up in my head suddenly rearranging itself to fit this new reality. She was unhappy, and the only thing I could do at this point was to man up and own it.

"I agree, and I know, and I'm so fucking sorry. But... I don't know if we can fix it." My voice dropped to a whisper. "I don't know if I want to fix it."

I held my breath, watching her face for a reaction.

We sat in more silence, both of us thinking, reflecting on everything that had transpired within the last 10 years of our marriage. At least, that's what I was thinking about. My gaze was downcast, staring at my hands as I picked a bit of rough skin from the edge of my fingernail. I hadn't realized Lily had moved to my side of the table until her warm hand landed on my arm. Looking up into her eyes, I could see the worry. A thousand things ran through my mind and I felt utterly defeated in that moment. A rush of failure coursed through my veins. I had failed her as a husband and I was failing Jordan as a father by telling his mother I wasn't sure if I wanted to fix things with her.

What kind of asshole was I?

I was ready to toss this entire life aside all because what? Because I had caught a glimpse of a girl from my past and had been hit with a bout of jealously? What the fuck was wrong with me? I was about to tell her that I was sorry and that I would do the things she needed me to do in order to make this work for Jordan, but she shocked me by letting her words spill first.

"Have you felt... No, never mind," she began before pulling her thumb to her mouth and biting the edge of her nail.

"No say it, Lily. We've already begun the conversation. Have I felt what?"

She hesitated, her eyes cast downward to her lap. "I just... do you feel like we made a mistake when we were younger? Rushing to get married when I got pregnant? Do you ever wish... I don't know."

"I don't regret marrying you, Lily. I don't regret any of my choices that I made for our family. I have regrets from my childhood, yes, but marrying you isn't one of them. You're my best friend. And this fucking sucks. Don't think for a second that this is the way I thought this conversation would go, but we both need to be honest with ourselves. It's long

overdue, don't you think?" My heart raged against my chest
as I struggled with the emotions that flooded me. There was
a part of me that wanted to take back my words and
continue to be in this marriage with Lily. It was the safe
choice. The easy path. The one that would continue to give
Jordan a childhood without a broken home. But the other
part of me knew that this wasn't the life I was destined to
live. It couldn't be.

"I think we both know that there has always been something missing between us. I think we both live with regrets
about some points of our past." She blew out a giant breath. I
watched her as she clasped her hands together, bouncing them
slightly in her lap. "I don't think I want to fix this either, Ry."
Lily's voice sounded strained as she breathed them into exis-
tence, her confidence wavering with the finality of them.

Her words replayed through my mind like they were inked
onto a ping-pong ball and someone was playing against a wall.

I don't think I want to fix this either.

She was giving me an out. She was giving *us* an out.

Amicably.

Without a fight.

Without tears.

Without *blame*.

The hole I had felt for so many years was not only
mirrored in her, but understood. Justified even.

Something's missing between us.

I stood suddenly, chair crashing backward behind me with
my sudden movement, and my arms scooped Lily into the
biggest, most fierce hug I had given her in what had to be
years. I spun her around, planting a kiss on her cheek. "I have
been tormented for so long Lily, feeling like the world's biggest
asshole because I wanted to be the man you needed me to be,
and the father that Jordan needs and deserves." I set her back
down on her feet, still holding her arms. "Why didn't you tell

me that you were feeling like this, too? How long have you been feeling like this?"

"Honestly? Because I thought I was just being selfish. You've provided us with such a beautiful life. You married me when we were barely able to comprehend what marriage was, just to do right by me and Jordan. I struggled hard with feeling like I needed to live up to *your* expectations... well, the ones that I created in my head, I guess."

I shook my head. "I'm so sorry, Lil."

She moved to sit at our table again, making herself comfortable. "You don't have anything to be sorry about, Ryder, neither of us do. We were just kids, forced to make grown up decisions. Sometimes things aren't meant to be. You've been my best friend for the better part of 12 years though, so I really hope we can continue that even if we're not always going to be together. We still have to be in each other's lives for Jordan."

"For Jordan, and for us too, Lil."

"So this is it? We've somehow managed to bypass a screaming match, the blame game, and an angry outburst? Ryder, I'm pretty sure this isn't how a normal break up conversation plays out. I'm pretty sure one of us is supposed to be blindsided here," she laughed, her hand coming up to rest under her chin as she leaned on the table.

"Since when have we followed the social norm?" I took a seat next to her, leaning back in my chair with my arms crossed. I kicked my feet out and studied my wife's features. We had always done things a little backward, a little outside of everyone's expectations. I had fully been expecting an argument tonight and the fact that we hadn't had one was a little unnerving. She clearly felt that, too.

"True, but I still feel like this conversation was too easy."

"A little, but doesn't have to be hard, Lil. Not when we're both on the same page about what we want."

She bobbed her head in agreement, looking down at her hands that she had moved into her lap. "Where do we go from here?"

"Wherever we want."

"And Jordan? How do we even begin to explain this to him?" she asked. Her bottom lip quivered while her eyes filled with tears again.

I pulled her into a hug, kissing the crown of her head as it rested against me. Our knees bumped together, and I held the back of her neck at an awkward angle, but I couldn't bring myself to let go. Not yet. "We tell him... gently. We'll sit him down, tell him how much we both love him, and each other, but that sometimes things just don't work out. We will figure it out, Lil. Together. I can promise you it won't be easy, but we will keep everything as normal as possible for him. You have my word."

She sighed heavily into my chest, burying her face in me. I felt overtaken by sadness as the memories of our life together flashed through my mind.

We remained in the dining room, both coming to terms with the conversation and what it meant for our family. It felt like the weight of the world had finally been lifted off my shoulders and I knew that we would not only survive this, but Jordan would ultimately have happier parents for it. Not only was there light at the end of the tunnel, but the whole damn tunnel seemed a little brighter, too.

CHAPTER EIGHTEEN

Elle

The days leading up to our high school reunion were relatively uneventful and mundane. For the most part, I went to work, came home, read, scrolled through TikTok, and would see Noah whenever we could. His work schedule had been crazy lately, but I was realizing more and more that I didn't mind just being in my own company.

It was Thursday night, our reunion looming less than twenty-four hours from now, and the weather had taken a turn for the worst. Thunder rumbled in the distance and brief flashes lit up the sky. The rain had barely started and was still a soft pitter-patter, lightly landing on the ground. I had always loved a good thunderstorm. I opened my front door and leaned against the frame, enjoying the smell of the fresh rain. Taking a deep breath, the cool air brushed my face—there was something about this weather that just cleared my head and enveloped my senses. I allowed my eyes to close while I focused on my breathing, trying to let all thoughts and worries leave my head. I stood still for many minutes, enjoying my weather inspired version of meditation. A gust of wind sent a chill through my body and I wrapped my arms around myself before closing the door.

I laid down on my chaise lounge and grabbed the blanket from across the back of my couch, pulling it up to my chin and snuggling in. My fingers curled around the remote as I tried to decide on whether I should watch something or get lost in a book. A yawn escaped, and I tossed the remote aside again, scooting myself further down the couch while reaching for my Kindle before I settled in, getting lost in the pages before me.

A BOOM of thunder startled me out of my sleep and I patted around on the couch, looking for my phone. The bright screen illuminated, and I tried to shield myself with the arm that was draped across my eyes. The clock read just after 11:00PM. My Kindle laid on my chest from where I had dropped it when I had fallen asleep. Rolling over, I tried to re-situate myself on the couch before thinking better of it and forcing myself to my feet.

Within seconds, I collapsed on the bed and snuggled into my duvet, not bothering to plug my phone in before I fell back asleep.

Soft kisses started at my ankle and slowly moved upward. I could feel him everywhere, tingles racing through my body. Rough hands moved hastily over my breasts, thumbs rubbing my peaked nipples in a delicious motion.

I was aching, panting, and desperate to feel him everywhere.

A moan escaped my lips, the sound encouraging him to continue nipping and sucking at my body. His mouth hovered over my core, hot breath panting heavily against my panties as I writhed below him, silently begging for his mouth on my sensitive flesh.

A gasp escaped me as I felt teeth scrape against my lower stomach and my eyes snapped downward to him, a wave of satisfaction rolling through me as I saw him biting at the edge of my panties, using his teeth to pull them off me. Once below my knees, I stopped watching, my head falling back to the pillow, back arching. I felt him rip them away at the same time as his mouth crashed against where I needed him the most, licking and sucking expertly, teasing me just the way he knew I liked it.

I could feel the climax building as my heels dug into the bed, his arm draped across my stomach, pinning me down as his tongue continued its rhythm. I looked down at him to find his eyes blazing, staring at me with a look of pure and raw desire. The look alone ripped a moan from my lips and my head crashed back to the pillow again as he began fingering me while still swirling his tongue on my clit. I was so close, I could feel the orgasm coursing through my veins...

A cry of pleasure escaped my lips as my eyes violently snapped open and I realized what had just happened. My hand was beneath my pajamas, fingers firmly in place on myself. I ripped my hand out of my pants and sat up, inching back until I was sitting up straight against the headboard.

I had just had the most realistic sex dream of my entire life, masturbated in my sleep, *and* orgasmed.

What.

The.

Fuck.

CHAPTER NINETEEN

Elle

S tanding at a high-top table, I subconsciously searched for him amongst the crowd, eyes bouncing from person to person. Noah had insisted that we come to our reunion, despite my last-minute protests and attempts to use every ounce of sexual leverage I could think of. Since stepping through the threshold of the banquet hall, my heart had not stopped beating wildly in my chest. Music played loudly through the speakers and the vibration seemed to keep time with my heartbeat, increasing my nerves with every changing song. The reunion was giving off prom vibes more than reunion vibes; I felt like I had stepped into a time machine. The banquet hall was crowded, and I shouldn't have expected anything less, considering who the crowd was. Our graduating class had always been very buddy-buddy with each other.

Sipping on a glass of white wine that was far too dry for my taste, I sighed deeply as the boredom creeped in and I let myself wonder if it had been an appropriate amount of time for me to now leave. I glanced over at Noah, who was speaking animatedly, hands and all, with a man I vaguely recognized. At least someone was enjoying himself.

Looking around the room, it was easy to see who was putting on a show for the sake of impressing others. Bored, I rolled my neck in an effort to make it a little less stiff and closed my eyes for a moment, enjoying the feeling of it pop a little.

Everything about this reunion felt so old school and lackluster that I was nearing my limit of people-ing for the night. Stick a fork in me, I'm done.

The exuberant laugh that bellowed out of Noah startled me; my eyes flew open, and I turned to see what on earth was so funny. Maybe this reunion was about to finally get interesting.

Before I could get my answer, though, the air was stolen from my lungs as I locked eyes with a familiar stranger across the room. A chill ran down my spine, and the entire room faded around me. I had convinced myself that I would never see him again, but as I stood frozen in place, my entire body was set alight.

He's here.

Ryder had the same piercing emerald eyes, though his hair had darkened slightly with age. His features were sharper than I remembered, more prominent, and tattoos peeked out from beneath the sleeves of his white button down. The cuffs of his shirt were rolled to almost his elbows, which showcased his strong, muscular forearms. I drank him in, unable to resist the pull toward him that I still felt.

I can't be certain how long I stayed like that, but I was jolted back to reality when Noah's heavy arm landed around my shoulders, forcing a knee-jerk reaction into looking up at him. His eyes were cast across the room, venom emanating from him as he tightened his grip on me.

When I looked back, Ryder was gone.

CHAPTER TWENTY

Ryder

I t was Noah.
Fucking Noah.
That's who she was with at the pub last week.

I seethed, anger radiating off of me as I paced the hallway just outside of the banquet hall. They were best friends in high school, and now they were, what? Together? They have to be after that pissing match, Noah just began when he put his arm around her, pulling her attention off me.

I had seen him in my peripheral and knew he was watching me as I stared at her. I could see a look of darkness painted across his face, but I refused to pull my eyes away from Elle. She looked stunning standing there in her royal blue dress and jean jacket, dark hair swept up slightly on one side with curls cascading everywhere, and those fucking red lips.

Nothing could have pried my eyes away from her.

She was beautiful, and I knew in that moment I was completely fucked. If she had married him... fuck. There was no way I was going to stop until I made her mine. I had sacrificed her for my entire adult life, and I was done. She would be mine if it was the last thing I did.

Once Noah threw his arm around her and she pulled her gaze away from me, I chose that moment to slip back into the shadows to reevaluate. Exiting the banquet room, I lingered in the hall to get my head together.

I needed to go speak to her, that's why I had come tonight, but I also needed a plan.

So much had happened since that night that I saw her at the pub—my head was still reeling and I was finding it hard to organize my thoughts. I leaned against the wall in the corridor, raking my hands up and down my face, willing my mind to process a coherent thought.

What I *wanted* to do was to go back in there and demanded she talk to me, but after that display Noah had just put on, I could see him and I having words and ruining any chance I had of talking to Elle tonight.

No, I had to do this right.

It was clear she was with Noah. I couldn't just go in all 'mister steal your girl' and throw her over my shoulder like a complete caveman. For all I knew, they were in love and had a solid relationship.

Shit, were they married?

I groaned, my head hitting the wall with a loud *thump,* at the same time I heard the *click* of the door a few feet away. My head whipped in the direction of the noise, eyes instantly connecting with bright blue ones. I watched Elle's perfect lips form an O as I took her by surprise; she hadn't expected me to be out here. She turned to leave, but I wasn't willing to miss my chance to speak with her.

"Wait," I said, my voice gruff but pleading.

She froze, saying nothing, her back to me. I could see the movements of her breathing in and out, her fingers grazing the door handle as she debated her next move. It was going to be an uphill battle, but I had wielded my sword, ready to fight for this girl.

"Talk to me, Elle..." My voice trailed off. I made no move to go to her, allowing her to have full control of the situation. It took every ounce of restraint in my body to not close the distance between us.

Turning slowly, she lifted her head to look at me. My eyes couldn't help but trail up and down her body, fully taking in the way she had changed over the years. My cock twitched in appreciation.

"What do you want, Ryder?" she said with defiance, her chin lifting in an attempt to come off strong. Uncertainty swam in her eyes. I wanted to take her against the wall and fuck the defiance out of her, show her that her facade didn't fool me. My breath caught in my throat and I struggled to find the words to say next.

What did I want?

Her.

I wanted her.

After all this time, after all these years. Still. Fucking. Her.

Did I say that? Of course I didn't.

That would be too easy, and apparently I was in the business of making my life much harder than it needed to be.

Speak words, Ryder.

Fuck.

We stared at each other, her eyes silently willing me to say something. Instead of opening my mouth to speak, my legs led me to her. Neither of us said anything as I approached, but a thousand things ran through my mind that I wished I could put into words. As I closed the distance between us, her eyes flashed with bewilderment, passion, and...fear. I planned to erase that look from her features permanently; she had nothing to fear. I was ready to make up for lost time.

When I stopped in front of her, our bodies so close that we were practically touching, yet the space between us still felt like miles. All I wanted was to pull her close, pin her to the wall, and kiss her until her breath became mine. But I couldn't, not yet.

"Ryder..."

A current of electricity seemed to flow through my veins and my heart suddenly felt like it weighed ten thousand pounds. "Do you feel that?" I asked.

She shivered, nodding once.

I watched as the goosebumps pebbled her skin and her nipples hardened beneath the silk of her dress. Licking my lips, I shifted my arm to lean against the wall above her head, my hips pushing forward and pinning her in place. Dipping my head, I leaned closer to her ear. "What if things had been different, Elle?"

I nuzzled my nose against her ear and could feel myself hardening against her. Her hot breath lightly panted against my neck. This woman was making me crazy, and I had been in her presence for five minutes. I was losing my control, and the unknown was eating me alive. I had to know if I could make her mine.

"Are you with him?" I demanded.

Moments ticked by, but I made no move to lift my head or shift my body away from hers as I awaited her answer; an answer she confirmed with every passing second. She shifted her face, our lips barely a breath apart.

"I..." she started, but stopped, turning her head away. I watched as her eyes snapped shut and her chest rose and fell in heavy breaths.

"Tell me to walk away," I growled. "Tell me it's been too long, that we can never be anything."

Her eyes snapped back to mine; a flash of anger danced across her beautiful face. She used the wall to push away, slipping under my arm to put distance between us. My eyes stayed pinned on her and I fought the empty feeling that washed through me.

"You were the one who said we could never be anything, Ryder. Ten years ago. I distinctly remember you coming to me, telling me that you were going to do the right thing and that *this,*" she gestured between us, "could never be anything!"

"Things have changed Elle, Lily and I — "

"No."

My lips slammed closed, understanding that in that moment nothing I could say would make her give me a chance right then. She thought Lily, and I were still happily married. She stared at me for a minute more, silently fuming, before walking back into the banquet hall, the door swinging shut without her sparing me a second glance.

A heavy silence filled the hallway and I couldn't decide if coming to this damn reunion was a huge mistake or my opportunity for another chance with the one that got away. It seemed like I had just fucked up my second chance. *Dammit.* I tugged at my hair, anger coursing through my veins as my chest heaved. I pulled my keys from the pocket of my jacket and headed out of the building toward my truck. Climbing into the cab, I shoved the key into the ignition and listened to the engine roar to life. I didn't bother waiting for it to warm up before peeling out of the parking lot. All I wanted was to get home to my crappy condo and figure out how I was going to deal with this. Nothing sounded better than my bed right now—I just wished I wasn't going home to it alone.

A FEW DAYS trickled by after the reunion and I found myself on autopilot, but it was my day with Jordan and I was determined to snap out of it and be present for him, at least for a few hours. It shocked me how quickly Lily had put things into motion after our discussion. Suddenly, it was clear how long she had been thinking about us separating; a fact that really should have bothered me more, but didn't. Not wanting to uproot Jordan or Lily, I had opted to sign a short-term lease at a condo owned by one of my clients. It was a shoebox, 2-bedroom, 2-bath with a crappy view of nothing, but it would be fine for me, and for Jordan when he was with me on my days.

Lily and I had agreed that to start, I would see him every Wednesday after school and have him every other weekend. We also agreed on an open-door policy where I could stop by whenever I wanted, pending a phone call first, and vice versa. We wanted to make this as smooth of a transition for Jordan as possible, and being that this was something Lily and I had both agreed on, I really hoped there wouldn't be a point where things turned ugly.

It was the Wednesday after the reunion and Jordan and I sat on a bench at the park, eating ice cream and catching up about our days. He was telling me a story about some kid at school getting hit in the face with the playground ball and how everyone was laughing at him, but he had helped him up from the ground and told the other kids to piss off. I smirked at his storytelling abilities, so adamant about how everything went down and so open to tell me all about it. He was about to turn ten and yet we still had a very open line of communication and a strong bond, despite the preteen attitude that was rapidly approaching. I observed him, studying his features and appreciating how much of myself and Lily I could see in him. He had my green eyes and Lily's nose, the dirty blond hair color that I had as a child, but Lily's soft curls, and a combination of both of our smiles. I reached over and ruffled his hair, which I knew he despised. He was getting too cool for that now.

"All right Jordan, finish up your ice cream and let's go shoot some hoops before I have to take you back to Mom's." My ice cream was gone, and the sun was starting to slowly set, casting shades of orange and pink into the sky. We only had a little more time left together before he needed to get back home so he could get ready for school tomorrow.

He side-eyed me at the mention of 'Mom's', scooping a huge spoonful of his ice cream and shoving it into his mouth. I expected him to say something, to ask questions, but instead he just hopped off the bench and went to toss his half-eaten ice cream into the trash.

"C'mon, Dad!" he yelled over his shoulder before running off toward the courts. I followed behind him lazily, pulling my phone out of my pocket and scrolling through my Facebook messages. My thumb hovered over Elle's name as I toyed with the idea of sending her a message. It had only been a few days since the reunion and I had been thinking about her nonstop. Elle had no idea that Lily and I had separated—she hadn't given me the chance to explain and it was eating me alive. The desire to talk to her was killing me.

I clicked her name, and our message exchange appeared on the screen. I stared at it for a minute before pressing the side button to darken the screen and pocketed my phone. Maybe I would find my balls later.

Stopping in front of Jordan, I slapped the ball out of his hand and dribbled it a few times before switching hands.

"Ready to get slaughtered, kid?" I laughed as he lunged for the ball. He was quick, but I was quicker, juking him and shooting my shot.

"In your dreams, Dad," he answered, just before the ball whooshed through the hoop.

———

LILY MET us on the porch when I dropped Jordan off and ruffled his hair as he passed by her. He shot her a look of disgust before running up the stairs.

"Bye, Dad!" he called, as he made a beeline to his room.

"Bye, bud," I said before turning my attention back to Lily. "What was that about?" I asked, not appreciating the way he had treated his mother.

"Don't ask," she told me, crossing her arms across her chest. "He's been giving me a lot of pushback and attitude lately. I think he blames me for everything." She looked down at the manila envelope she held in one hand, bringing my attention to it. I bit the inside of my lip, watching her shift on her feet.

"I'll talk to him," I told her before nodding my chin in the direction of the envelope. "What's that, Lil?"

"Um, I had the separation paperwork drawn up if you want to look over it and get back to me on everything." She picked at an invisible piece of lint at the bottom of her sweater.

"Okay... that was quick," I stated, a little shocked that she had drawn up papers so quickly.

Then a realization hit me like a ton of bricks. "Holy shit, is there someone else, Lil?"

"I... um... no, Ryder, there's no one else. I mean, I have been talking to someone as of recently, but there was never anyone else before we decided to split."

I stared at her skeptically. She had never lied to me, but something wasn't sitting right. Sensing my doubt, she moved to me, reaching for my hand.

"I swear on Jordan's life, and you can look through the phone bill and my Instagram messages if you want reassurance. We barely started talking three or four days ago."

I nodded slowly, taking her word and the papers.

"I'll look these over and get back to you in a few days. If everything looks fair, I'll sign them and we can get the process started."

I waved the envelope in the air before turning to head back to my truck.

"Ry," she called, sadness thick in her voice. I stopped

walking but didn't turn around. I wasn't sure how to feel in that moment—I just felt nothing. "I just want you to know that I would never betray your trust, and I loved you. I *love* you. It was always just you, and I didn't anticipate talking to someone this soon. It just kind of happened. But it did *just* happen, and I need you to know that."

"Okay, Lily." My hands balled into fists as I closed the distance to my truck. Throwing open the door, I slid into the familiar seat and tossed the paperwork down before cranking the ignition, the engine roaring to life. My hands slammed against the steering wheel with too much aggression before I turned the wheel and began to drive. I couldn't pinpoint why I was so upset, I only knew that I was. It was a lot to process in a short amount of time. Seeing Elle, our exchange at the reunion, now this with Lily.

Lily talking to someone else was a *good* thing. It meant that it was now my chance to pursue what I wanted. To pursue who I wanted. And you know what? There was no fucking time like the present.

I thrust my hips into the air slightly to allow room to pull my phone out of my front pocket, while keeping a grasp on the steering wheel as I drove. Tapping on the Facebook Message app, I quickly found her name, and sent her a message which demanded her address. I made a mental note to get her phone number as well. Within three minutes, she had messaged back.

Good girl.

Inputting her address into my GPS, I drove straight to her house, plan be damned. I was going to just show up and see what happened. Because why the fuck not?

CHAPTER TWENTY-ONE

Elle

I stared down at my phone in disbelief for several minutes, long after the screen had gone dark.

Ryder was coming over.

Why?

I knew I responded to his text message way too quickly. I was too desperate to see him again, and I couldn't figure out why I was doing this to myself.

Isn't this what I had successfully avoided for over a decade?

Isn't this exact moment the one that I knew would break me, so I had done everything that I could to make sure that it would never happen?

Then, in a matter of seconds and a text message later, it was all about to come crumbling down.

The knock at my door came too fast. I pushed the side button on my phone to illuminate the time—it had been less than fifteen minutes, which means that there was no way that he wasn't on his way over when he messaged me. He would have never made it from Shadow Hills to my house in that short amount of time.

For a split second, I debated on not answering the door. If I simply didn't open the door, then the guard around my heart would stay safely secured. If I didn't open the door, he would eventually just leave and we could both go about our lives and pretend like we had never even seen each other last week.

But we had, and now he was out front of my house, knocking again.

"Elle, please let me in." His voice came through the door muffled with a hint of defeat. I counted to thirty in my head as an effort to slow my racing heart, before taking a deep breath and pulling the door open. The walls around my heart softened as I took in his appearance. Meeting the gorgeous shimmering emeralds of his eyes, I inhaled a breath as I momentarily got lost in them. Still so beautiful, filled with unspoken words and emotion, this time there was something more. Something I couldn't quite pinpoint.

He entered my studio, taking in the small space. His scent surrounded me. Aftershave, pine, and sawdust filled the air, even though it was clear he wasn't wearing his work clothes. I let my eyes flutter shut as I mustered up the courage to speak. When I reopened them, he was staring back at me, so I gestured over to my small couch.

We sat by the fireplace, him on one end of my sectional couch and me on the other. The magnetism between us begged me to scoot closer, but I refused. I needed to keep a clear head, and everything about him clouded my senses.

Time passed slowly as we sat staring into the fireplace, the tension in the air building with each passing minute. Stealing a glance, my breath caught as the firelight illuminated his face in a warm glow. He raked his fingers through his hair and down his face, letting loose a guttural growl.

"Why do you keep doing this to me, Elle?"

"What?" I breathed, the air barely making it up into my throat for me to produce the word.

"Pulling me back in. It's been years. Fucking *years*, and not once have you left my thoughts."

His words crashed over me like an ocean wave, drowning me before I even knew what was happening.

"I've tried to be a good man, a *family* man, but you were always there, creeping into my thoughts and making me feel like I made the biggest mistake of my life, putting someone else before myself." He scoffed and shook his head. "Two someone else's, actually. Jesus, I'm fucked in the head."

Processing his words, I stood and started pacing in the space between my couch and the kitchen. It had been years, yet here we were in front of each other, unresolved feelings surfacing faster than an oncoming tornado. What could I even say? Was there even anything *to* say? This was all happening too fast, and I felt like the weight of the world was sitting on my chest.

I stopped pacing and faced away from him, staring toward my small kitchen while biting my thumbnail nervously, a habit that I had since I was a child. I sensed his presence behind me, but I didn't turn. He was so close I could practically feel him, but he wasn't touching me at all. His fingertips brushed my shoulder blade, and I finally spun around to face him, forcing myself to be confident and hold my head high.

"You chose her," I breathed, looking into his eyes, feeling like the wind was being knocked out of me.

"I chose her for our kid, not because I wanted her." The angered tone of his voice made my stomach drop. "I was going to break up with her and then she told me she was pregnant. What was I supposed to do?"

I threw my hands up, frustration bubbling. "It doesn't matter, Ryder. She's still your wife, and I chose Noah."

"You chose wrong," he growled, grabbing me softly by the neck and pushing me up against the door, our lips so close they were practically touching. I stopped breathing, a primal sense of need washing over me as he stood close, breathing heavily. His nose brushed mine and my eyes snapped closed. I had to stay strong. This wasn't the hill I would die on; I wasn't a home wrecker and Lily had been my friend once upon a time.

I pushed him away, my push weak and my willpower even weaker.

"You need to leave. This can't happen. Not now."

"But this *will* happen Elle, mark my words. You. Will. Be. Mine. I'm done sacrificing having you for what isn't even the right thing anymore. There are things you don't know." His eyes burned with more unspoken words that he wasn't letting fall from his mouth. I stared at him with my lips parted, mentally begging my legs to move me further away from him.

"Please Ryder," I whispered, "you need to leave."

I pulled the door, holding it open while staring at the floor.

He stepped toward me and placed his strong fingers beneath my chin, tilting my head upward so that it forced me to look at him. His eyes darkened, burning deep into my soul.

"This isn't done. It's barely just beginning, Elle."

He released me and stepped through the doorway. Once he reached the bottom of the porch, he turned back, giving me one last heated look, spilling everything that had been bottled up inside of me over the last ten years: longing, passion, lust, and a broken heart that was begging to be whole.

CHAPTER TWENTY-TWO

Elle

I couldn't help but feel like I had betrayed my best friend as I walked into Noah's place, heart hammering and body soaked from the rain. After Ryder left my studio, I grabbed my keys off the table, peeked out my window to make sure I could no longer see his truck, then dashed out of the door to my car.

I felt guilty, so incredibly guilty, and like I had cheated. I obviously had not, but the feeling of shame had washed through my still shaking body as I had stood there, staring at my door, replaying everything that had just happened in my head. There was no doubt in my mind that I needed to go to Noah. I needed to talk to him and get everything off my chest.

I knew it would hurt him.

He loved me and had loved me unconditionally since we were children. I knew that by me admitting that after all this time I still had unresolved feelings for Ryder; it was going to sting. Noah didn't deserve that, but he also didn't deserve a girlfriend who felt so much for another man.

It was a double-edged sword, one that was sharp on one side and dull on the other, and I couldn't decide which was more painful. A sword that cuts swiftly is less painful than one that takes effort into achieving the cut. I knew that in some aspects this would be a swift cut to our relationship, severing it in an instant as soon as I admitted what was happening inside of my heart and my head, but it would also be like using a dull blade, cutting through each individual strand we had worked so hard to rebuild. I wasn't sure I was ready for that.

Although, if I were truly being honest with myself, I knew we couldn't keep being placeholders for each other just because it was convenient and comfortable. It was time to put it all on the line. The cards had been dealt and I knew the second that my eyes connected with Ryder's at the reunion that my life would be flipped upside down. I just hadn't realized the gravity of the situation until tonight when Ryder showed up at my studio to talk.

As if the heavens above knew the turmoil within me, the skies opened up the second I left the safety of my car. A cold, violent rain beat down upon me, soaking me to the bone as I made my way to Noah's door. Thankfully, it was unlocked and I quickly slipped inside, pausing to let my eyes adjust to the environment.

Noah was sitting at his kitchen table, a small glass of whiskey in one hand and his phone in the other. The room was dark and the phone illuminated his face. I could see a scowl painted across his handsome features, and he didn't glance up as I shrugged off my coat and laid it across the bench by his front door. He seemed lost in his thoughts and I couldn't help but wonder if he somehow already knew.

Approaching him slowly, I wondered if he realized that I was even there.

"Hey, No..." I let the thought trail off as I assessed his reaction. I didn't want to startle him, although the darkened look in his eye as he stared at his phone was unsettling. His eyes snapped up to mine at the sound of my voice, and he instantly set his phone facedown on the table.

"Ells!" he replied, too cheerfully. He opened his arm to the side so that I could slip onto his lap, and I did so, easily falling into old routines as I hugged him tightly around the neck. I shivered, still chilled and wet from the rain. He breathed deeply, inhaling my scent as he squeezed me back, not seeming to mind that I was getting his clothes wet too.

I pulled back from our hug and slid into the chair beside him, wanting to talk to him at a little further distance. "Noah, I think we need to talk..." My voice trailed off again, and I suddenly doubted whether or not I wanted to have this conversation right now. I took a deep breath and let it out slowly, willing my nerves to calm.

He stared at me with an expression on his face that I couldn't quite read. I licked my suddenly dry lips and stared down into my lap, trying to plan my next sentences. Noah sensed my nerves; he reached over and pulled my hand into his, stroking his thumb over my knuckles in a soothing motion.

"Elle..." he spoke, his voice low. His eyes were cast down, staring at our hands. "Go to him."

Shock radiated through my body, my heart dropping into the pits of my stomach. I looked at him in disbelief, convinced that I had heard wrong.

"Wha...what?!" I stammered, searching his eyes for clarity.

After a moment he spoke again, his voice slightly louder and more firm. "You heard me, Elle. Go to him."

I pulled my hand away from him like he had lit it on fire.

"I...what?" I rubbed my temples, processing his words. My breath was coming in heavier and I involuntarily shook my head. I was so confused. "Go to him," I repeated slowly, testing the sentence out on my tongue. It tasted foreign and wrong.

He nodded slowly, my eyes transfixed on the bobbing motion of his head indicating that I heard him right.

"I'm not going to pretend like I didn't know this day was

coming, Ells. I figured it would happen a lot sooner than this."
He took a deep breath. "I saw the way you two looked at each
other at the reunion."

I sucked in a sharp breath, nearly choking as it lodged in
my throat. Noah paid no attention to my dramatics. I eyed
him skeptically, suddenly pieces of an unsolved puzzle clicked
into place as I stared into the face of the man I had been
learning for years.

Suddenly, memories came flooding back to me. Noah in my
car staring angrily at his phone, refusing to tell me who it is,
Noah and Lily arguing when they thought no one was listening. I pressed my hand against my mouth, analyzing every
detail of what I've been missing for years, scrutinizing his
behavior just now—it was the same as it had been all those
years ago.

"You're talking to her again." It wasn't so much of a question, as it was a fact. I watched his eyes widen slightly, briefly,
before he slipped right back into the hardened mask that only
a cop knew how to wear so well. He wasn't letting his features
tell me anything.

"You were never actually mine, Elle. So now I'm telling you
to *go to him.*"

I stared at him for what had to be several minutes before I
found my voice to speak again. I was fighting an inner battle of
feeling relieved and even happy for him, but also feeling a
little...hurt. How long had this been going on under my nose?

My eyes narrowed as I stared at him with disbelief.

"Noah," I began, my voice sharp. "Answer the question. Are
you and Lily talking again?"

"Barely. We have exchanged a few text messages." He
couldn't meet my eyes, but I felt the truth in his words. He
was still hurt, clinging onto the past just like I was. "For the
record, I don't think they're married anymore."

"She said that?"

"No, she didn't. It's just a hunch." He turned his attention to his empty whiskey glass, wrapping his hand around it. I watched the movement of his finger as he tapped it on his glass, trying to give my mind a minute to process. The longer I sat in silence, the angrier I became.

"So, what? You and Lily text a couple of times and suddenly you're pushing me back in Ryder's direction? You're not upset, Noah? You're not going to get angry, or yell...feel betrayed? You're just throwing in the towel that easily?" I realized my voice was raising but I couldn't stop myself. I was lashing out and spiraling quickly.

He wasn't even going to fight for us.

Did I want him to?

Was I so disposable that he was just willing to send me on my way and be done? Would there be friendship after this? I couldn't lose him again. I wouldn't. But...if he had cheated? *Had* he cheated?!

Fuck that.

Noah knew that I was seeing red and pulled me to my feet, his huge arms wrapping around me and hugging almost painfully tight, but I wasn't done being mad. My body was shaking, so enraged and overwhelmed by the cyclone of emotions that was spiraling inside me.

He nuzzled into my hair, his lips pressing against my head as he spoke again. "Elle, it's because I love you that I am telling you to go to him. I'm not an idiot and I could *see* that he still wants you. I'm not angry, because I am your best friend, Elle, and I know how much you have tried to shove your feelings for him down into the deepest part of your soul and lock them away. For years. You've done that for years. Aren't you exhausted?"

I nodded my head in his chest, scowling because I equally hated and loved that he was right. "I am too," he continued. "I know that you have put everything into our relationship, and I hope you can see that I have too, but there was never *really* an us. You and I? We've been best friends since we were three, minus a few years of our little hiatus, and yeah, the sex has been good, but you can't sit here and tell me that you have the same types of feelings for me as you do for him. Are you going to look me in the eyes and lie to me right now? *Lie to both of us?* Think about it, Elle." Kissing my hair, he loosened his hold on me, pulling back to look me in the eyes. "I'm giving you this out because we both know that this relationship of ours has been a drawn-out friendship with benefits."

Tears blurred my vision. He was right—and I had no doubt that he had been faithful during our time together. He was simply telling me the ugly truth that I had tried so hard to deny myself for the better part of a decade. We both still pined for the two people who had no choice but to push us both away because of circumstance.

"I'm sorry," I whispered, burying my head back into his chest.

Just before the sobs racked my body I heard him whisper, "I'm not."

CHAPTER TWENTY-THREE

Elle

It had been over a month since the night my world came crashing down around me, leaving me crawling through a pile of ash, trying to navigate my way out.

Ryder had gone radio silent, not even so much as a text message had been sent. I tried not to let it bother me; he was a married man, after all. At least, I think he is. I could only assume that Noah's assumption had been wrong. If Ryder and Lily had split up, wouldn't he have shown up again by now? Noah told me to go to him, but I couldn't bring myself to do it. If they were still married, I refused to be the one to come between them. I couldn't face that rejection. Instead, during the last four weeks, I have spent every waking moment over-analyzing. I've picked apart the entire reunion, when he showed up at my house, and my breakup conversation with Noah.

Noah and I had ended things in a romantic aspect but had fallen back into a comfortable friendship that I was grateful for. After a lifetime of friendship and months of dating, I was terrified that it would all be gone the moment we said goodbye to our relationship. Although it did take us each a few days to move past some awkwardness, we were able to flip through the chapters of our relationship and pick the pen back up to continue writing the story of our friendship. I had always known Noah was a good man, but it was in these last few weeks that I was able to see just how special he was. My head was still reeling over the fact that Noah and I slipped into a relationship and back out of it without any added drama, but when I really stopped to think about it, it made sense. If someone is truly meant to be in your life, they will be.

My daily routine stayed consistent, albeit a little mundane, but lucky for me, I had a firecracker as a best friend who always knew how to make me laugh.

The sun sat high in the sky as the days stayed lighter for longer now, and I cradled my phone between my shoulder and ear, listening to Rosie go on and on about the newest bad boy in her life. Fumbling through my purse while I walked to my car, the coolness in the air prickled my skin. I shivered at the same time as I found my keys and I adjusted the phone so that I was holding it again. My eyes scanned the parking lot of my office, keeping an eye out as I continued toward my car.

"Elle, he's just so... so... infuriating! Maddening. He thinks I am some damsel in distress. Seriously, he's there every time I turn around," Rosie ranted through the phone.

I laughed. "It sounds like he's..."

"A freaking stalker? Yeah, I know."

"Protective. The word I was going for was protective."

"Protective of WHAT?! I don't need a man to protect me. I can slay the monsters on my own, you know that."

"I know that, and you know that, but does he?" I rounded my car, approaching the driver's side. The keys fell from my hand as I gasped in surprise.

Weaved through the handle of my door was a single red rose.

"Elle? Elle, are you okay?" Rosie yelled through the phone.

"Yeah, I'm okay. I'm good. There's just..." I held the phone to my ear, my body twisting as I looked around the parking lot. Aside from a few cars, it was deserted—I was the only one out here. I bent down to pick up my keys, shoving them into the pocket of my coat. "There's a rose in the handle of my car door."

"A rose?" she questioned.

"A rose," I confirmed.

"Well, who's it from?"

"Hang on, there's a note." I reached over, grabbing the small tag hanging from the rose that was tied on with a piece of twine. The word '*Mine* ' was scrawled across it in masculine handwriting.

"Elle? What's it say?"

"It says 'Mine,'" I whispered, lost in thought. There was no doubt in my mind who this was from... but why now? It had been a month.

Rosie squealed in excitement, and I pulled the phone away from my ear. "Mine? He just inscribed the note with MINE!? Girl. You're totally fucked. Both in the mental and literal sense. That man is going to dominate you in the bedroom."

I groaned, sliding into the driver's seat and locking the doors. "Why does everything have to be so dirty with you, Rosie? This means nothing. I haven't heard from him since he showed up at my place a month ago. Plus, *he's married.*" I emphasized the married part, my tone going sharp. She was completely shipping me and Ryder, but was forgetting that huge detail. It wasn't going to happen; he was a married man.

"You sure about that, Elle? Just based on what you've told me about his character, he doesn't seem to be the type of man who would pursue someone while being married."

Pressing the speakerphone button, I let the phone drop into my lap before running my fingers through the ends of my hair, thinking about what Rosie had just said. She had a point.

"I don't know…"

"Seems like it's your move babe, are you going to take the King or keep dancing around the board?"

I let my head fall to the steering wheel, albeit a little too hard. I winced, pain searing my forehead. "Shit," I mumbled, rubbing the throbbing bump.

"I have to go Rosie, love you," I told her before abruptly ending the call. I wasn't normally one to hang up on my friends, but I couldn't handle her energy right now. She would want to continue to push me into hunting him down and taking charge of the situation, but I needed to think.

She had a point. What if he wasn't married anymore? But to that, I had about a dozen burning questions. I rubbed my fingertips over the growing bump on my forehead, trying to soothe the pain, while closing my eyes for a moment as thoughts swirled around my head.

Right now, the only thing I knew for certain were two things: I was irrefutably still in love with Ryder, and I needed time to sit in my thoughts and decide how to handle this situation I suddenly found myself in.

CHAPTER TWENTY-FOUR

Elle

Three days later, there was a featherlight knock on my door. It was the middle of the day and I wasn't expecting anyone, so I finished the page I was reading before placing my bookmark inside and setting the book down on the couch. Unlatching the deadbolt of the door, I opened it slightly, peering through the security screen. The sunlight was blinding, but I could make out the silhouette of the man who I had so desperately tried to push out of my mind over and over again.

"Ryder?" I called, opening the screen and stepping out onto my small porch. His back was to me, already walking away from my house, but he stopped when he heard my voice. "What are you doing here?"

He turned, eyes sweeping over me.

A wave of embarrassment and nerves hit me like a wrecking ball. I was standing before him in an oversized tee shirt, my most worn-out pair of 'mom jeans', and hair tossed carelessly into a messy bun—yet his eyes flared with desire. My stomach flip-flopped, his look alone undoing me from the inside out.

Raising an eyebrow, I cocked my head, attempting to come off as calm, cool, and collected while I waited for his response. Striding toward me slowly, he closed the distance between us. He was staring me down like a lion stalking his prey, but stiffened when his gaze landed on the bruise on my forehead.

"Who did that to you?" he growled, his eyes darkening.

I brought my fingers to my forehead, flinching at my own touch. Ryder's hand lifted to cover mine, his rough fingertips trailing over the bump, sending a jolt of electricity through my body. I stepped back, needing the distance. "I did. I hit my head."

He searched my eyes, seeking out the lie. I stared back at him with ferocity, not backing down.

"Why did you leave me that rose, Ryder?"

He looked at the ground, his fingers raking through his hair. I learned years ago that this was his tell. Ryder was nervous. I guess we had that in common. "Look Elle, things aren't how you think they are."

"No, Ryder, they're exactly what I think. You're marri—"

"No, Elle. I'm not. Lily and I are legally separated. The divorce will be finalized whenever the courts finish up the paperwork. It's done. *We're* done."

My eyebrows pinched in thought. "Why? When?"

"It's been over for a long time now. We started the process before I even saw you at the reunion," he explained, taking a step toward me again. "Look, can I just come inside? We can talk. I'll explain everything. Answer every question that you have."

My body betrayed me as I felt my head nodding. Spinning on my heel, I began walking back toward my studio, holding the door open so Ryder could walk through. Once inside, he sank into the cushions on my sectional couch, his arm draping across the back. I sat opposite of him, the feeling of déjà vu setting in. "Why?" I repeated myself, bracing for the impact of his words.

"Because I've been lying to myself for the last ten years, and it's fucking exhausting."

I was fighting the war between the angel and the devil on my shoulders, each sending rapid-fire questions through my mind. "Lying to yourself about what?"

"About not wanting you," he responded simply, as if it were the easiest thing in the world to tell me this. "I wanted you then, and I want you now." His fingers drummed on the back of the couch as he watched me, waiting for a reaction or a response.

I swallowed hard, choosing my next words carefully. "You left her... for me? You left your family for me?" I was asking a question I wasn't entirely sure I wanted the answer to. It couldn't be true, because if it was, it solidified all of my fears; I was a home wrecker. *I never asked to be a home wrecker.*

"No. I left our marriage for me. But I will *never* leave my family. Lily and Jordan will always be a priority in my life."

I exhaled, watching as Ryder looked into the distance across my small studio. Painted across his face was truth, confliction, pain, and vulnerability. He was telling me the truth, and I could feel myself starting to cry. The raw emotion that was radiating off of him was stifling all of my senses.

"The last ten years with Lily were comfortable. Beautiful. They were happy, Elle. We raised our son, all three of us growing up together. We were children who were forced to become adults, and we only survived because we had each other to lean on. I don't regret the choice that I made, but there was never a day that went by where a part of me didn't still feel empty. I think I always knew what that emptiness was, but I forced myself not to let myself go there. Then I was forced to admit it to myself when I saw you at the pub a couple of months ago."

My hand flew to my mouth. "You saw me at the pub? When?"

"Yeah," Ryder said, chuckling softly. "I fucking saw you and I panicked. I ran out of there like a little fucking girl. You were with some guy. I didn't know who then, but it was Noah."

I giggled, a vision of Ryder hightailing it out of the restaurant vivid in my mind. "You could have said..." My voice trailed off as I stopped myself from finishing the thought, instead looking down and picking at an invisible piece of lint.

He couldn't have said hi, and we both knew it.

Ryder grunted knowingly, and I could feel him staring at me again. Watching. Judging my reaction to all he was saying. I felt him move closer to me, our bodies now just inches apart.

"Are you with him?" he asked, repeating the question he had asked me at the reunion. I lifted my eyes to meet his, taking a deep breath.

"No," I said firmly. "Not since you—"

The words were lost as he crashed his lips into mine. His hand moved quickly to cradle the nape of my neck as he leaned into me and stole my breath. I parted my lips and his tongue found mine, dancing together feverishly as my eyes sealed shut, praying this wasn't a dream.

"Elle..." he groaned, his hand skimming down the side of my body.

The sound of my name on his lips set me off. My body ignited, burning only for him. I had never felt this level of need, so hypersensitive to his every touch. His rough hands gripped my waist, pulling me on top of him and positioning me so that I was straddling his lap. Though fully clothed, I could feel everything as my center rubbed against his hard length. A soft moan escaped past my lips and he broke our kiss, pulling back to look at me, his eyes darkening. His grasp on my hips intensified as he pulled me lower, moving my body against his.

My eyes slammed shut as the friction became almost too much. It was driving me wild.

"Ryder," I panted, "are you..."

I believed his words, but I needed one last ounce of reassurance.

His hands flew up to my face, knowing what I was asking without me saying the words. He kissed me roughly, owning my mouth before tearing his lips away and looking into my eyes.

"It's done, Elle. I wouldn't be here if it wasn't."

"Okay," I said, nodding. He pressed his lips to mine again in a soft kiss. I sighed into him, and my hands wandered across his chest, admiring the muscles hidden beneath his soft cotton tee shirt. My gaze traveled down his body to the area of skin where his shirt had ridden up, granting me a view of his lower abs, v-cut on his waistline, and the tattoos he kept hidden beneath. A smile pulled at my lips as I tilted my head, kissing him again while his fingertips trailed a path up my back, fisting my hair. Our kiss began tender and slow, and it felt like we were exchanging small pieces of our hearts through each touch. It was clear how much this meant to both of us.

Ryder's mouth began its descent toward my neck, sucking and nipping at the soft skin, the feeling making me squirm with anticipation. My head fell back as he swirled his tongue on my flesh, pulling a moan. My whole body felt alive and needy for his touch.

I wanted more.

I craved it.

"Ryder, please..." I begged, leaning forward to run my tongue up his neck as my hand wandered toward the bulge in his pants.

Catching my arm, he lifted it to his mouth and kissed the inside of my wrist.

"Don't start something you aren't ready to finish, Elle.

Once you give me the green light, I won't hold back. I've fantasized about this moment for the last ten years. There will be no holding back."

I pushed my legs further into the couch to lower myself, rubbing my center along the ridge in his pants. "I want this, Ryder, so bad."

In one swift movement, we were standing, and he was moving us toward my bed. With my legs wrapped securely around him, I resumed licking and teasing his neck as he carried me. He groaned as he tossed me onto the mattress. I shifted to adjust myself on to my arms, leaning back as I watched him under hooded eyes. My breath caught as he hoisted the hem of his shirt over his head, exposing his chiseled body and exceeding every mental image I had ever had of him. I felt my core clench, alight with anticipation, as he tossed his shirt aside. A coy smile spread across my lips, and I openly stared at his body with appreciation.

Years of manual labor looked good on him.

He crawled toward me on the bed, his hand reaching for my shirt. "Off," Ryder told me, and I quickly pulled the shirt over my head. "Bra too."

I did as I was told, my eyes never leaving his. Reaching over the bed, I dropped it to the floor and smiled up at him from under my lashes.

"Good girl," he said as he leaned forward, pulling my nipple into his mouth. Struck with sensitivity, he was awarded with a moan while my hand flew to the back of his neck to hold him in place. He nipped and teased my nipple before releasing it from his mouth and blowing a cool breath of air on it. As he continued to tease it with the pad of his thumb, his mouth found my other nipple and continued the delicious torture.

"Ryder... please... I... need more..." I panted, my head flew back to the pillows. He began kissing his way down my body, alternating between sucking on my flesh and blowing cool breaths of air onto the sensitive spots.

Grabbing the blankets to brace myself, the fiery need for friction pulsated through my veins. My center was throbbing, begging for attention. Ryder slowly undid the button of my jeans and pulled everything off in one movement.

Lying bare before him, I instinctively bent my legs at the knees, creating a wall that obstructed his view.

"Now is not the time to get shy, sweetheart." He pried my legs apart, and they fell to the side, leaving me wide open for his viewing pleasure. He wasted no time dipping a finger into my desire before pulling it out and examining the shine that coated his finger.

"So fucking wet for me," he groaned before licking his finger clean. "And so fucking sweet."

Whimpering, my back arched as he inserted two fingers into me. The hunger burned in his eyes while he watched his fingers pump into me.

"I could watch my fingers disappear into this sweet pussy all day, but I've been fantasizing about my mouth on you for years. I'm going to devour you now, and I want you to stay still. If you're still, I'll let you come quickly. If you move, you'll be forced to wait. Understand?"

I tilted my head further into the pillow, my body quivering with white hot need. With my senses on overdrive, there was no room for overthinking his words. All I could process was the fact that this man was about to make me lose my mind. I had never been so turned on.

His mouth hovered above my center, and the feeling of his breath caused me to shiver as I bucked my hips, desperate to fill the space that was between me and his lips.

"You do understand that you're being told to stay still, right Elle?" He chuckled darkly.

"Yes, just fucking... *please,* Ryder." I was so tightly wound, I was on the verge of self-combustion.

His mouth connected with my warmth as he licked expertly, tongue moving up my slit before nipping gently at my most sensitive spot.

I moved beneath him, my eyes so tightly shut that I was seeing stars as he toyed with me relentlessly.

"I told you not to move," he growled, pulling back and nipping at the inside of my thigh. He sat back on his heels, fingers trailing lazily up and down the inside of my thigh. My skin tingled with every caress, a fire sparking with every movement.

"Ready to try again?"

I nodded my head, my eyes still closed. "Yes."

"Good girl."

I gripped the pillow, his praise making me melt further into the bed. Ryder calling me a good girl did something to me I had never known I would be into. I never thought I'd have a slight praise kink, but I felt myself grow wetter at his words.

My body hummed, crying out as he slammed a finger inside of me at the same time as his mouth connected with my clit. I clenched around him as a second finger joined the first. Holding his other hand firmly on my lower belly, I had no choice but to fight against my desire to move, which only proved to build the ecstasy faster. My body wasted no time climbing toward release.

Ryder removed his hold on my stomach and my back arched just as the climax ripped through me, a tsunami of pleasure coursing through my body while I screamed out his name. Collapsing onto the bed, fully satiated, I looked up at the ceiling, a smile spreading across my face.

"How do you want me?" I asked, watching Ryder sheath his length with a condom.

"Oh beautiful, the better question would be, is there any way that I don't want you?"

Gripping the back of my knees and scooting my body to the very edge of the bed, he leaned down, touching his lips to mine. My legs wrapped around his waist and I could taste myself as he deepened the kiss, lust pouring out of him. He lifted my hips higher and aligned himself with my entrance.

"The answer to which is no," he said, slamming into me in one thrust. He circled his hips, his hardness filling and stretching me, fitting me perfectly.

"You feel fucking amazing," he groaned, pleasure thick in his voice.

He continued to command my body in ways I never could have dreamed of. He alternated between a slow, soft torture to rough and demanding, teasing my body and pulling it back to the brink of another orgasm.

"You're getting close again."

I nodded in agreement, eyes rolling backward in sweet oblivion.

Gripping my hip, he pulled back slowly before driving into me again. He continued this pattern, reaching between us to rub my clit with his thumb. I clenched around him as the euphoria began to overtake my body.

"I'm going to... I'm..." I panted, grabbing the wrist of his arm that held my hip.

"Come. Do it now."

Digging my heels into his firm ass, I screamed out, my orgasm crashing through me.

Placing one hand above my head, his fingers laced with mine, Ryder continued to pump into me faster, finding his own release before collapsing on top of me.

Lazily, he kissed my neck as he caught his breath.

I skated my fingers up and down his back, memorizing the feeling of his skin against mine. His shoulder blades squeezed together at my touch, and he bit my shoulder gently. Reaching between us, he pulled himself out of me, leaving me empty and spread out before him.

Walking toward my tiny bathroom, I watched as he removed the condom and knotted it before wrapping it lightly in a tissue and dropping it into the trash can.

"Where do you keep your washcloths?" he asked, turning on the faucet to let the water warm.

"Second drawer down."

He opened the drawer and pulled out a small pink wash-cloth, holding it under the stream of water until it was soaked, then rung out the excess.

Moving toward me, the mattress dipped as he sat down and placed the cloth between my legs, cleaning and soothing my sensitive center. Grinning up at him, a blush warmed my cheeks and I could feel shyness creeping under my skin.

"Thank you. That was..." I laughed, looking away, searching for the word. "That was unlike anything I've ever experienced."

He brought his hand to my cheek, cupping it and tilting my face to look at him. He rubbed his thumb over my lips. "That was only just the beginning, Elle. We have ten years of lost time to make up for."

Catching his thumb between my lips, I sucked on it roughly. "Ten years is a lot of time Ryder, we better get started."

"Oh, we will, but first, get dressed."

He leaned down, scooping up my shirt and bra from the floor, and tossed them next to me. "You're going to need suste-nance for what I have planned for you. It's time for our first date."

"First date?! But... no, Ryder! I... look at me! I'm a mess."

He grabbed my hand, lacing his fingers with mine, and pulled me up to stand. "No, you look beautiful. And thoroughly fucked. Now, off to the shower, you go." Spinning me around toward my bathroom, he smacked my butt playfully and gave me a little push to walk.

"Will you be joining me?" I asked, pouring as much seduction as I could into my voice, feeling a little awkward about trying to be sexy. But as I glanced over my shoulder, I found him watching me, his length hardening again. He fisted himself, licking his lips while his eyes trailed down my body.

"No, beautiful, if I join you now, the only thing I'll be eating tonight is you. Again. Now go."

I play pouted and started off to the shower again, letting the water get hot before stepping into it. Once inside, I turned the water hotter and watched as the swirls of steam rose around me.

I just had sex with Ryder freaking Thompson and now he was about to take me on our first date.

Eighteen-year-old Elle was high-fiving twenty-eight-year-old Elle, the feeling of Ryder's touch lingering on my body.

CHAPTER TWENTY-FIVE

Ryder

I stared up at the yellowed popcorn ceiling of my crappy condo as I laid alone in my empty bedroom. The moonlight streamed in through the open curtains, forcing me to shield my eyes with my arm. Images of Elle raced through my thoughts as I tried to push them away so that I could get some sleep. Instead, I thought of dark hair cascading down her bare back, the feeling of her flesh as my nails bit at her soft hip dips, and how amazing it felt to finally sink into her for the first time.

I felt myself growing hard and reached down to adjust myself in my shorts. Tossing the pillow over my head, I groaned and mentally begged the sandman to come. It was nearing two in the morning and my day would be starting in less than three hours, not nearly enough sleep to function as a contractor.

But this woman was all-consuming and finally within reach of truly becoming mine. As a teenager I would lay awake and think of her, and here I was, a man pushing thirty, doing it all over again.

The term high school sweethearts trickled into my

thoughts, but that's not what we were. We were high school star-crossed lovers, forced apart when the pull was so strong. I took pleasure in the fact that all of that was irrelevant now— she was back in my life and there was no chance in hell I was giving her up again. I would fight through any obstacles, take down anyone or anything standing in the path of us finally getting our chance. She was *mine*, and this time I wasn't letting her go.

ME: **What time is your lunch break today, beautiful?**
 ELLE: Whenever I want. I usually go around 11:30 or so. Why?
 ME: You'll see.

I looked down at my watch and realized I had only thirty minutes to finish my mission and make it into Ridgewood before Elle went on her lunch break. It'd be tight, but worth it.

"Order for Thompson!" the short woman behind the counter screamed, her accent thick. As I approached, she held the bag filled with Styrofoam boxes up and watched me slip a ten into the tip jar. She beamed up at me as I removed the bag from her grasp and started toward the door, the scent of hot Mexican food wafting up and making my mouth water. After jogging back to my truck, I jumped inside and started the engine as quickly as I could. I leaned over to place the food on the floorboard before pulling out of the lot, speeding through the back roads between Shadow Hills and Ridgewood. I was racing against the clock to get to my girl.

I made it with less than a minute to spare, flying into the spot adjacent to hers and killing the engine. Grabbing the bag and the bouquet of roses I had bought earlier, I hopped out of the truck and went over to her car. Leaning against it, I could hear her squeal as she walked toward me from her office building.

The sight of her stole the breath from my lungs. She wore a red skirt that flowed around her in the breeze, and the white top she wore left little to my imagination. But what really did me in was the bright red lipstick that made her lips irresistible. I couldn't help but picture them around my cock.

Setting down what I was holding onto the hood of her car, I snaked my arm around her waist as she approached and pulled her close to me.

"I like this," I growled, gesturing at what she was wearing. I peppered a trail of kisses from her neck to the top of her shoulder, wishing I could go much lower than that.

A giggle slipped from her glossed lips as my frisky hands roamed her body.

"Well, thank you! What are you doing here?" she asked, pulling away from me, her curiosity piqued. She hadn't noticed the food or flowers on her car.

"I brought tacos."

"Tacos!" she said animatedly, her eyes sparkling in the sunlight. "You sure do know the way to my heart."

She stretched her arms toward me, bouncing in place, excitedly waiting for her food. I chuckled at how clearly food was the way to this girl's heart, placing the flowers in her hands instead.

"OH! Wow, Ryder, these are stunning. You didn't have to do this."

Leaning forward, I kissed her cheek, just before scraping my teeth against her earlobe, making her shiver. "Yes, I did. One of the perks of being mine."

"Oh, am I yours now?" she teased, eyes flashing with mischief and desire.

I attached my lips to her neck and sucked hard, pulling the soft flesh into my mouth before letting it go again, marking her faintly. "That shouldn't even be a question in your mind. Is it?"

She looked away shyly, although I could see right through the shy girl act now. Tucking a piece of hair behind her ear, she looked up at me with her perfectly round blue doe eyes. "No."

"Good. Now, eat." I thrust the box of food in her direction, her fingers grazing over mine as she took it. Popping the tailgate down on my truck, we ate side by side. She told me a story about her co-workers that were trying to sneak around with each other, but were so obvious that the entire office knew. I told her about my plans with Jordan for later that evening. It was my night to have him, and we were going to grab some burgers before our weekly ritual of playing basketball until the sky grew too dark to see.

"Can I make you dinner Saturday night?" she sing-songed. "It's my turn to spoil you, and I make a mean lasagna."

"Lucky for you, I've been craving lasagna."

She smiled brighter than the sun that was scorching us with its heat.

"Great. Six o'clock Saturday then." She checked her watch, hopping down from the tailgate. "Oh shoot, I'm going to be late getting back. Thank you for all of this. You're the sweetest."

She stood on her tiptoes to place a kiss on my cheek. As she began to pull back, I caught her by the neck softly, pulling her back and capturing her mouth. I swept my tongue against hers while I held her body between my legs tightly. When I released her, she was breathless, a flush of color covering her cheeks.

"A kiss on the cheek is for friends. Last time I checked, friends don't feast on your pussy like I did the other night, do they?"

Her eyes went wide, staring at me, and I tossed my head back, erupting in a roar of laughter. It was fun watching her react to my filthy words. The best part was this side of me had been reserved for her and she didn't even know it.

"I'll see you Saturday, beautiful." Placing my hands on her shoulders, I spun her body and smacked her ass, encouraging her to start walking back to work.

Her laughter carried through the air as she sauntered back toward her building, sashaying her hips and putting on a show for me. I enjoyed the view, eyes never leaving her ass as she entered the building and out of my line of sight.

CHAPTER TWENTY-SIX

Elle

Ryder's crude words reverberated through my mind as I worked, layering the ingredients of my lasagna into a Pyrex baking pan. Lasagna was about the only thing that I felt confident enough to cook for him; my cooking skills still severely lacked in every other recipe. The anticipation of tonight had me on edge. As I lifted my wineglass to my lips and took a healthy chug, I thought about everything that I planned to lay out on the table tonight. He could spend every day and night learning my body, bringing me food, and calling me his, but underneath the surface is a girl that I'm not always confident in, and he needed to meet her. I wanted to start at the beginning and dig deep — go back to high school, and rip back open the wound that I fought so hard over the years to close.

We needed to talk about that day in the woods, the stolen moments, and about what was said between the flames on the night of graduation. We weren't kids anymore and if we were really going to give *us* a fighting chance, I couldn't see a way to avoid having this conversation. I placed the glass back onto the counter, stem cradled between two fingers, and zoned out, overcome by my thoughts.

The sound of the oven startled me, sending my glass to shatter on the floor. I cursed as I crouched to pick up the broken glass; the universe working against me when I sliced my thumb on a jagged piece of glass. Blood instantly seeped from the cut, and I felt like I couldn't breathe. I was so overwhelmed by literally everything—my anxiety had been triggered to the point where I knew I just need to ride it out. Sliding down to a full seated position on the floor, I let the tears flow out of me as I sucked on the cut on my thumb. My eyes eventually fluttered closed, and I rested my head against the cabinet behind me.

Hearing the front door open, I rushed to wipe away the fallen tears from my cheeks.

"Elle? Hey, I'm here," Ryder called, entering my home and closing the door behind him.

"I'm down here," I said, forcing myself to sound upbeat. He stepped closer and immediately found me, rushing to my side while assessing the broken glass and spilled wine. His eyes followed the mess to the thumb I still had in my mouth. Plucking it from between my lips, he looked at it, kissing it softly.

"Are you okay? What happened?" He tugged me to my feet, pulling me flush with his body to wrap me in a hug.

"YOU happened, Ryder," I exploded, pushing his chest as I backed away from him. I needed the distance, finding it hard to breathe. Part of me knew I was misdirecting my anger, that he just stepped into this situation. The weight of everything else wasn't his fault, but I also didn't care. The pain of the past lingered in my body, and it seemed as though I had reached my breaking point. A tear escaped, landing on the floor between us.

"You fucking hurt me. So bad. Ten years ago. You burned me and scarred me, and I've never fully recovered from that."

He winced, his face contorting into pain and regret. "Elle... I," he stumbled for the words, caught off guard.

I moved to turn, but he caught me by the wrist.

"I'm sorry, I... you didn't deserve that, Ryder."

He pressed his lips to mine, choking my next words as he moved me backward, hoisting me up and placing me onto the counter. He wrapped my hair in his fist, softly pulling my head back as he forced me to look in his eyes.

"I won't apologize for the decisions I made when it comes to my family—when it comes to Jordan. Without taking that path and choosing *him*, I wouldn't be the man I am now, standing here in front of you. I will not apologize for that. But I will apologize for how I handled shit with you."

He leaned his forehead against mine, and I closed my eyes, choking back another set of tears.

"I didn't know you at all then. I only knew my attraction to you, and I knew you were what I wanted, and what I felt for you bordered on obsession. When I made the decisions that I made, I was selfish and sought you out for closure for myself. I didn't consider what my words were doing to you. I honestly thought you would just walk away and forget about me." He caught a loose tear that had slipped down my cheek, wiping it away with a swipe of his thumb. "I thought I would forget about you, too."

He kissed me again, softer this time.

"I never forgot about you," he whispered. His voice was barely audible over the pounding of my heart.

I nodded my head, his words thick in the air as I thought about everything he had just said, and what he hadn't said.

"I really am sorry I blew up on you just now. My anxiety has been coming and going in waves today. When I broke my glass and cut myself, I... well... everything crashed down around me."

"You don't ever need to explain yourself to me."

"But I do. How I acted just now was a little unhinged."

Lacing his fingers through mine, he lifted our hands to his lips and kissed my knuckles, his eyes never leaving mine. My stomach rumbled, ruining the moment.

"Crap. And I forgot to put the lasagna in the oven. Are you starving? It needs at least forty-five minutes. Should we order a pizza instead?" I was rambling and feeling guilty. "I'm so sorry."

Saying nothing, Ryder glided through my kitchen, placing the lasagna in the oven and setting the timer. Once our food was cooking, he grabbed my hand, pulling me off the counter, and guided me to the couch. He pulled me into his lap as he sat down. I leaned my head against his shoulder as he began to play with the ends of my hair. I felt my anxiety wane as I focused on the rise and fall of his chest. We sat quietly for a long time, neither of us making any motion to break the silence, until finally I decided it was time to ask a few lingering questions.

"Why were you in the woods that day?" I murmured against his collarbone. He stilled, the weight of his hand weaved through my hair, suddenly gone as he dropped his hand to the couch cushion.

"I followed you."

"Why?"

"Because I was consumed by you. I saw you leave campus, and I needed to know where you were going."

"And when you found me? What was your plan, then?"

He grunted. "I don't know. I didn't have a plan. I just wanted to be near you, even if it was from afar."

I contemplated his words, looking up at him to study his features. "If I hadn't run, would you have kissed me?"

"Yes," he stated, a smirk pulling at his lips. I bit my lip to stop myself from smiling.

"You had a girlfriend. *My friend.*" I narrowed my eyes at him for good measure.

"I know. I had planned on breaking up with her, though. You were who I wanted."

Taking a deep breath, I leaned into him again, inhaling his scent and wrapping my arms around his middle. I was at war with myself on whether I wanted to hear all of this. Rehashing the past was reopening the wounds, and I suddenly felt like I would rather just put it behind me and move forward. I was so conflicted.

"Elle, you have to understand. I was eighteen, fatherless, and trying to do the right thing by my kid. My father didn't do the right thing by me, and I was terrified of ending up like him. I sacrificed something that I wanted more than I wanted the air in my lungs, for my son, but I always kept you—the memory of you, locked tight and hidden. I never forgot about you, despite knowing that I should. I forced myself to push you out of my thoughts for Lily's sake, but our marriage was over long before we decided to separate. It was only after seeing you at the pub that I really let my thoughts wander back to you and let myself fantasize what my life could be like with you in it. And now that I have you, I'm not letting you go for anything. Ever. So when you feel like you need to scream at me? Scream. Want to hit me? Beat the shit out of me. I probably deserve it. I'll take any piece of you that I can get, the good or the bad."

The fact that he didn't hold back in telling me everything spoke volumes about the type of man that he had grown to become. I hated that our paths had parted, but was beginning to see that maybe all of my pain had been worth it. My eyes grew heavy with unshed tears and I could feel the final piece of brick around my heart come crumbling down; a finality to it that brought me a new sense of hope.

"Say you'll give me a chance to make it up to you?" he asked, his voice low, his eyes sparkling down at me as he brushed away a piece of hair that had fallen onto my face.

Life was complicated, but he was what I wanted. He always had been. It was time for me to put everything on the line. I bounced up to kiss the corner of his mouth. "Of course I will, Ryder. I've lived my life without you and there's always been a piece of me missing. You make me feel whole."

His fingertips caressed my thigh. "Oh beautiful, you have no idea."

CHAPTER TWENTY-SEVEN

Elle

The next few weeks passed beautifully and blissfully as Ryder and I spent every moment that we could getting to know each other in ways that we were never given the opportunity to in our past. On the nights that Ryder wasn't with me, he was with his son, and I absolutely loved that about him. Seeing the pride that radiated out from him whenever he spoke of Jordan and told me stories about their adventures together never ceased to bring a smile to my face. He thought that their bond had only gotten stronger after the separation, which made him more optimistic about the divorce and their future with co-parenting. I, on the other hand, still felt sick to my stomach at just the thought of their breakup. I knew I hadn't been the cause of it, but everything still seemed so fast, and I was waiting for the other shoe to drop. Could he really be in a place where he was ready to jump into a new relationship with me? Was he well and truly over her? Had he had the time to be on his own and explore what he truly wanted? He swore he was, and he showed me constantly, but I still couldn't help but let the fear and anxiety creep in.

The sounds of whispers in my ear amplified my insecurities while I laid in bed on nights he wasn't with me, and all the doubt set in. I forced myself to bury it down and ignore the devil on my shoulder. As time passed, it was getting easier to trust his word and for the first time; I was picking me... *us*. I wanted him, and I refused to let anything get in the way of that, even my biggest fears.

Rosie and Noah both did their best at talking me off the ledge when my thoughts ran away with me, although I always treaded lightly when I spoke to Noah about my relationship with Ryder. Whichever way you looked at it, Noah was still someone that I had been involved with on a romantic level, and it didn't feel right venting my current relationship fears to him. He was tight-lipped about *his* love life, so I tried to mirror that behavior and not completely open up about mine.

Rosie, on the other hand, had pried every single detail out of me and continued to hound me for more information whenever we spoke. She claimed she was living vicariously through me, but we both knew my life was certainly more vanilla than hers was. Well, until recently, anyway.

"WEAR SOMETHING CASUAL, but that'll make me want to throw you over my shoulder, carry you to my truck, and fuck you senseless." Ryder's deep voice reverberated through the speaker of my cell phone, and a blush crept onto my cheeks as I bit my lower lip.

"Right, I'll put on my best turtleneck and high-waisted jeans then!" I bantered, my voice coated in sweetness and feigning innocence.

He grunted in response. "See you at eight," he told me before ending the call. I let the phone slip from my grasp and into my lap before inwardly squealing.

Tonight, Ryder was taking me to a new bar that had just opened, Andromeda. According to Rosie, this was, and I quote, "the hottest new bar in town, but also a little rough around the edges." I wasn't entirely sure what she meant by that, but my curiosity was piqued, and when I casually mentioned it to Ryder, he insisted we go check it out.

Glancing at the clock, I saw it was already almost six o'clock and my grumbling stomach reminded me if I was going to be drinking tonight, that I needed to eat something first. Walking over to the pantry, I assessed the shelves, debating on what to eat, and decided that the simplest thing would be pasta.

I popped my AirPods in and set to work on my meal while listening to a 'hype playlist' on Spotify that Rosie had sent me, readying myself for the mindset of going out tonight. Swaying to the beat of Britney's "I'm a Slave 4U", I allowed melody to overtake my body while I stirred my pasta at the stove.

Abandoning the wooden spoon in the pot, my hands weaved through my hair as I seductively moved my body lower to the floor, dancing for myself, my confidence increasing and making me feel sexy. As I worked my body back into a standing position, a strong arm wrapped around my waist. Panic flooded my body, and I spun in place, coming face to face with Ryder. His face was lit with a lustful smile, his eyes dark with desire. I ripped the AirPod from my left ear, panting heavily, still struck from terror.

"What the hell Ryder, you scared the absolute shit out of me," I snapped, pushing him away from me with both hands. Removing the other AirPod, I set them on the counter and scowled at him. "Well?"

"I wanted to surprise you, treasure," he responded airily, lifting a shoulder. "I didn't mean to scare you. I'm sorry. I didn't realize you had your headphones in."

I assessed him through narrowed eyes. "Treasure? Where did that nickname suddenly come from?"

"Because you're a treasure." He took a step closer to me. "And I'm a pirate."

I laughed, rolling my eyes at him with a smile playing on my lips.

Apparently, the man has jokes now.

Ryder took another step, closing the distance between us. I could feel my body ignite, humming with need. My core clenched tight as my eyes dropped to his mouth. All I wanted to do now was kiss him.

"And I want this booty," he said. His large hands squeezed my butt, hoisting me up in one fluid movement.

A burst of laughter erupted out of me as I instinctively wrapped my body around his. He began his assault against my lips as he walked us toward my bed, keeping one hand firmly against my butt while the other moved up my back to the nape of my neck. He held me, kissing me punishingly before laying me down on the edge of the mattress. His fingers found the button of my jeans and he tugged them off and wasted no time before dropping to his knees in front of me, pulling my panties down slowly.

"Ryder, the —" but I lost my thoughts as he ran his tongue up my slit, before turning his attention to the sensitive bundle of nerves that craved him the most. Shoving a finger inside of me, he continued to tease me in delicious strokes.

"So wet. Always dripping wet for me, Elle."

I clawed at the bed, fisting the comforter tightly as my back arched. A moan escaped my lips as he continued to flick his tongue against my clit. My hands moved to the back of Ryder's head, holding him in place as I quickly climbed toward the brink of my orgasm. "Ryder," I panted. "Close, so close."

He abruptly pulled away and flipped me over like a rag doll

before pulling me onto all fours. "Oh, no you don't. The only way you're coming right now is on my cock."

I peeked over my shoulder and watched him remove his shirt with one hand. He dipped a finger into my throbbing heat, swirling it around before adding another.

"Do you like that, baby?" he asked, his voice husky.

My eyes were fixated on his movements, watching as he pulled a condom from his back pocket. He ripped the package open with his teeth before rolling it down his length. I felt myself clench with anticipation.

"Tell me how badly you want my cock."

He didn't give me the chance before plunging into me, drawing another moan as a response. He held my hips as he slowly pulled back, before driving into me again and again.

"You're so tight. It's like you were made for me, Elle. So fucking perfect." He suddenly pulled out of me completely, resting back on his heels. "Lay down, beautiful."

I did as I was told, turning my body so that I was lying on my back and I spread my legs, giving him an open invitation to do whatever he pleased. He leaned down to trap me in a punishing kiss as he dragged his finger through my wetness again, smearing it all around my entrance. Fisting his cock, he lined himself up and entered me, filling me completely.

He groaned, lips breaking free from our kiss. "The way you fit around my cock is like heaven on Earth. We were made for each other, Elle. There will be no one else for me in this lifetime or the next. You're mine." He pumped in and out slowly, while my fingernails dug into the back of his neck, moans falling from my lips like music notes. His motions became faster and rougher the harder my nails nipped his skin. The sounds of our lust filled the air and pushed me closer to my release.

"You're about to come," he told me, slowing his thrusts,

reaching his hand between us to circle my clit. The stimulation too much for me to handle, and as if his words were the key to my undoing, my climax washed through my body.

A scream tore past my lips as the water from my pasta boiled over and sizzled against the hot stove.

CHAPTER TWENTY-EIGHT

Elle

Pulling into the parking lot of Andromeda, I looked around at the obscene amount of motorcycles that lined the front rows of the lot, mouth agape as I mentally guesstimated more than fifty total.

"Um, Rosie failed to mention that this was a biker bar..." I trailed off, glancing over at Ryder.

"I don't think this is a biker bar, but it looks like they're scouting it, for sure."

"Scouting it for what?" I questioned, feeling suddenly nervous. Ryder reached over and pulled my hand into his, searching my face.

"Just as a place to hang out, Elle. It's okay. Do you not want to go in?"

I shook my head. "No, no, it's fine. I just get nervous in new situations. I can tell this place is going to be a lot different from Reggie's and the pub, that's all." A lump formed in my throat as anxiety threatened to take over. Closing my eyes, I focused on my breathing while I unlatched my seat belt and opened the truck's door. Meeting Ryder at the back of his truck, he lifted my hand to his lips and gave it a gentle kiss.

Two bouncers waited outside of the bar; one checking IDs while the other held a clipboard and pen. I fumbled through my purse looking for my ID, an embarrassed smile coating my lips as I mumbled to myself and silently promised to invest in smaller purses in the future. Finding it, my arm jutted out to show the guy that I am, in fact, over the legal drinking age. He said nothing as he stepped aside, allowing us to move toward clipboard guy. Using one burly arm, he pushed the door inward and left just enough room for us to cross the threshold.

Andromeda was absolutely gorgeous. It had a dark and modern vibe, and everything was black with hints of silver playing into the little details. Music played at the perfect decibel: loud enough for the vibe to hit just right, but not so loud that you can't hear the people you came with. The most impressive thing, however, was the ceiling. No matter where in the building you looked, glittering stars were looking back down at you, twinkling and tempting you with their secrets.

Mesmerized, I could feel my feet moving as Ryder guided me through the building to the bar. He kissed my temple before sliding onto his barstool and waiting for me to do the same.

"What do you want to drink, treasure?" he asked, lifting a hand to wave the bartender over, a smirk pulling at his lips as he used my new nickname. I rolled my eyes at him but couldn't stop the smile that pulled at the corner of my lips as well.

"Rum and Coke please," I told the bartender, before returning my attention back to Ryder. My eyes traced his strong jawline, admiring the way the stubble lined his jaw. I reached out to touch it, my thumb caressing over his lips as I did.

He caught my hand and pressed a light kiss into my palm. A soft moan escaped me as a jolt of electricity ran from his lips straight to my center. "If you don't stop tempting me Elle, I will make good on my suggestion of taking you to my truck to fuck you senseless."

"You wouldn't dare," I teased. "A white knight is always a gentleman."

"Careful — you never truly got to know me when we were young. I may come off as the white knight, but when it comes to you, I most certainly feel like the villain. You make me wild. Possessive."

He caught me in a searing kiss, showing me just how possessive I made him feel. When he pulled away, Ryder's eyes were dark. The effect I had on him made my desire pool, and I knew I was soaked for him. *Again.* His hand was on my thigh, the contact of his skin on mine making me heady. He leaned his body toward me, whispering in my ear.

"Are you wet for me again, Elle?" He slipped his free hand under my skirt and toyed with the edge of my panties. A shiver ran through my body.

I nodded my head a little too enthusiastically. "Yes."

"How wet?"

"Soaked," I said quietly, biting down on my bottom lip. Without warning, he was moving my panties aside and plunging two fingers inside of me, curling upward to hit that delicious spot that no other man had found before. I gasped at the same time as he whispered, "Shhhh."

My eyes rolled to the back of my head as I bit my lower lip to keep myself from moaning.

"Right now, my body is shielding you from everyone in this bar, Elle; no one can see you except for the bartender. How good is your poker face?"

My eyes moved around the bar, the worry creeping in. I couldn't just let him finger me in the middle of the goddamn bar—but as his thumb began its delicious torture on my clit, I could feel my resolve crumbling. I kept an eye on the bartender while he distributed drinks to customers, praying he would stay at the other end of the bar. I bit down harder on my lip to keep quiet as Ryder continued working me hard and fast beneath my skirt.

"That's a good girl, Elle. No one has the faintest idea that I'm fucking you with my hand right now, do they?"

I whimpered in response, my body instantly feeling like a flamethrower had doused it, and I could feel the orgasm building quickly within me. My walls clenched around his fingers. My release was near. Ryder curled his fingers once more at the same time as he circled my clit with his thumb, and suddenly my body vibrated with tingles as I teetered on the edge.

"Come for me Elle, do it now," he whispered, warm breath tickling my ear in the most sensual way. I was pushed over the edge, free falling into the darkness, and I bit down on his shoulder to stop the scream that threatened to tear from my lungs. A chuckle shook from Ryder's body as he turned to kiss my temple, removing his fingers from inside of me. My legs snapped shut, the reality of what we had just done sinking in.

"You came before our drinks did, my love." He smirked, licking his fingers clean. I stayed silent, overwhelmed by the array of emotions that currently plagued my body.

A few moments later, the bartender placed our drinks in front of us, and I drank mine down in three big gulps.

SETTING my empty glass on the damp napkin in front of me, I stifled a yawn, sitting back in my chair, my eyes growing heavy. Ryder's arm was lazily draped across the back of my barstool as he downed the rest of his bourbon in one go.

"Ready to leave, beautiful?" he asked, raising his arm to flag down the bartender again. "Or can I order you one more?"

"We can go. I'm already two drinks ahead of you," I said as I pushed the empty glass further away from myself.

"Only because I'm driving."

I grinned at him. "I know, such a white knight."

"Only where it counts." He slipped off his barstool and kissed the side of my head, an endearment of his I was quickly growing spoiled by. "I'll be back. I'm going to hit the men's room." He tossed his credit card on the bar. "If he comes over, have him run this."

I watched as he walked away, my eyes trailing after him. I could see the other women turning to watch as he passed, a few whispering to their friends and discretely tilting their heads toward him. My cheeks flushed and I couldn't help but wonder if they were enamored by how handsome he was, or if they somehow knew what we did on this very barstool earlier this evening. Just before he was out of sight, I felt the presence of a large body slide into the chair next to me. My eyes tore away from the hallway that Ryder had disappeared into, and over to a familiar face.

"Hey there, gorgeous, you come here often?" the man teased. His voice was familiar, and when I turned to face him, it mildly shocked me to see who it was.

"Oh wow! Hey Mi—Matt! How are you?" Leaning forward, I wrapped my arm around him in a quick, awkward side hug.

"I've been good. Work's been busy, but it's nice to get away from the grind and check out this new spot. Is it your first time here?" The smile on his face was genuine, ever the nice guy.

"Yeah! Quite the vibe change from Reggie's, though, huh?"

"It is, but I prefer the atmosphere at Reggie's. I seem to have good luck over there." He winked, his eyes trailing down from my face to my cleavage and back up again. He didn't even try to hide the smirk as he licked his lips and stared at me like he was ready to pounce. I was struggling to find a way to respond when I felt his hand land on my thigh. "Are you here with a friend?" he asked, gazing around the room.

"Uh ya, and he should be back any second." Nerves ricocheted through my soul, setting off alarm bells. I couldn't bring myself to move his hand, that was still caressing my thigh. "It was great to see you, Matt." My tone was sharp, and I prayed he would take the hint and walk away.

Spinning on my barstool, I stared ahead and pretended to be more interested in reading the names of the various bottles of alcohol on the wall in front of me. My elbows rested on the bar and I leaned forward, willing my nerves to rest as Matt's eyes felt heavy on me, predatory. Matt's personality shift was making me feel extremely uncomfortable. Finally, he stood from the barstool, taking a lock of my hair between his fingers before placing it behind my ear.

"It was great to see you, Elle." His fingers trailed down the side of my cheek before dropping to my shoulder and sliding along the side of my boob. I sucked in a sharp breath, my head snapping toward him as I prepared to go to battle for myself.

Who did he think he was?

Before I could get the words out, though, he was already walking away. My eyes shifted from his back and landed on Ryder's face. A shiver ran down my spine as I watched the anger rage through him as he stalked toward me.

"Who the fuck was that?" he demanded, his voice thick with venom.

Instinctively, I leaned back slightly in my chair. My mind couldn't catch up with the emotions. "Just some guy I met a few months ago at another bar. He came over to say hi." I wasn't sure why I was downplaying what had just happened, but the look of fury that washed over Ryder's beautiful features froze me in my chair.

"Just some guy," he repeated slowly. "And what exactly did *some guy* want?"

"To say hi Ryder, like I said."

"It didn't fucking look like he was just saying hi. He had his hands all over you, Elle."

"Yeah, I know, and I tried to get him to leave, but he wasn't taking the hint," I spat, my own anger now coursing through my veins. Was he seriously getting mad at me for this?

"Have you fucked him, Elle?"

My mouth fell open in disbelief. "I... what?"

"Have. You. Fucked. Him," Ryder seethed.

If this was a fantasy novel, he would have shifted into his dragon form and breathed fire into this entire establishment.

The anger that radiated off him scared me, and I suddenly realized what he had meant when he said that with me, he was the villain. I wasn't sure I liked this side of him.

I continued to stare at him, too stunned to even respond. A steady stream of curse words flowed through my mind as I glared into his dark eyes, when suddenly he turned and retreated out of the bar, leaving me sitting there. My hand flew to the bar for the credit card that was still sitting on top of it, and I bolted after him. My body quaked a with desperate frenzy, unsure of how to think, feel, or react to everything that was currently playing out.

Cool air hit my face as I pushed through the double doors and I jogged toward where we had parked the truck. I stopped walking as Ryder came into view and watched him rage a war against himself. In a smooth motion, his fist collided with the door of his truck, bending it beneath his impact. He beat into the door a few more times before his fist dropped and he stood still, shoulders sagging and head moving slightly with each rise and fall of his heavy breaths.

I approached slowly, taking his bloody hand in mine to look over his wounds. He was banged up, but nothing that would require actual medical attention.

"Ryder…" I said, my voice trailing off, unsure of what to say next.

"Don't."

"Ryder, he meant nothing."

"Don't."

"It was months ago."

"I said DON'T," he boomed, causing me to drop his hand. The harshness of his tone making me feel small. "I should have never asked."

He turned to face me and gone was the anger in his eyes. Sadness had taken its place. Guilt and remorse washed over his features as he slowly searched my eyes. I could read him like a crystal ball, but no amount of guilt and sadness could deflect from what had just happened, how he had *reacted*. In a matter of seconds, he had made me question everything.

"Get in the truck Elle, let me take you home," he spoke, his voice barely above a whisper. I nodded once and walked around to the passenger side of the truck, sliding onto the bench seat and securing my seat belt. I stared out the window as he started the truck, the engine roaring to life and sending gentle vibrations throughout the cab. Only when we exited the parking lot and were surrounded by darkness did the silent tears flow over and stream down my face.

I kept my gaze out the window throughout the drive, never daring to look over at Ryder, but I felt his eyes on me continuously. He slowed to a stop in front of the home that my granny unit was nestled behind, cutting the engine and turning in his seat to look at me. I continued to stare blankly out of the passenger side window, not having the energy for whatever he was about to say. When he reached over and pulled my hand into his, I let him, closing my eyes as he rubbed his thumb softly over my knuckles. He lifted my hand to his lips, pressing a soft, apologetic kiss to it, and the butterflies in my stomach started to flutter. I ignored them.

"Look Elle, I'm sorry. I've never had jealousy rage through me like I did when I saw that guy put his hands on you. It was everything I could do not to walk over and bash his head against the bar. I've never..." I could feel him looking at me and I fought the urge to squirm in my seat. "You make me feel feral. Like I have no control. *Absolutely fucking insane.* I haven't felt this way since I was eighteen and secretly pining for the nerdy girl who drove me wild."

My eyes narrowed as I looked over at him. Him circling back to how he felt about me in high school was like salt to the wound with this fight. My body was tingling with adrenaline, fighting against unspoken words, knowing that anything that came out of my mouth from this moment on would surely make our night worse.

Desperate for an escape, I reached for the handle and pushed open the door, hopping down from the truck and closing it roughly behind me. Walking down the unlit path to my studio, I wrestled with every fiber of my being to not turn around and look back at the truck.

He didn't follow—he didn't come after me, and it made my shoulders sag even further.

Ryder still hadn't started the engine as I slipped inside of my home and secured the deadbolt. Leaving the house dark, I drifted over to my bed and laid my head against the feather soft pillows. The scent of him was everywhere in my studio and it made it so much worse. I slammed my eyes shut while my heart beat wildly in my chest, my mind betraying me and only thinking of him.

I wasn't afraid of his jealousy or even the way he reacted. What scared me was that his mind immediately put the blame on me for another man's unwanted advances. He didn't grant me the opportunity to explain that not only was I not interested in Matt, but I was *uncomfortable* in his presence tonight. Instead, Ryder's insecurities led him to the assumption that I had asked for Matt's attention, and that was what devastated me the most. It *hurt*. It showed his lack of trust and confidence in me.

Laying on my bed, I buried my head into my pillow and fought the tears that were threatening to fall. Pictures of Ryder and me over these last few weeks swirled through my mind like a movie projected from my heart. Things had progressed so quickly between us, it really shouldn't have surprised me that the other shoe had dropped. I just hadn't been expecting it to hurt so badly once it did. My eyes grew heavy, and I tried to focus on my breathing. Squeezing my eyes together tightly, I snuggled into my bed as much as I could, praying I would just pass out before the anxiety swallowed me whole. A million things ran through my mind as my heart finally steadied.

"I don't want to fall in love with you," I whimpered to myself, just before sleep overcame me.

CHAPTER TWENTY-NINE

Ryder

Pacing my dark bedroom, I stared down at the stained carpet my landlord didn't bother replacing, as the entire night replayed in my head. I was so enraged about everything that had happened, and I felt like a fool. The moment I stepped out of the men's room, my eyes instantly found Elle from across the room, only to find *him* sitting in *my* chair, touching *my* woman. She was *letting* him touch her.

I watched as she turned her face away from him, but made no move to remove his hand. My fists balled up at my sides and it had taken every fiber of my being not to walk right up to the guy and rip his head off.

I had forced myself to stay back.

To watch.

To see how this exchange played out.

And I didn't fucking like what I saw.

It had been a mistake asking her if she'd fucked him. I shouldn't have. I didn't *need* to. The answer was obvious by the way he pawed at what was *mine*, but the words flew out of my mouth before I could stop them.

Foolish. I have been so incredibly dim-witted when it came to this woman. For so long, I had been stagnant in my relationship that I have completely forgotten how to act when it comes to a new relationship. Hell, I never even really had the chance to learn how to act in a new relationship, considering how young I was when I met Lily. I felt like a fish out of water, and I didn't fucking like it.

I should have followed Elle after she stormed out of my truck, but my anger held me back. I had apologized for my behavior, and she tossed that apology back at me before slamming the door in my face. How was I in the wrong here? I wasn't the one who let some girl have her hands all over me.

What provoked me the most wasn't the past relationships, or even that she had a run in with one of them. It was that she was *mine,* but she was still letting someone else touch her.

No one fucking touches what's mine.

Maybe I should have followed her into her house. Should I have continued to push for a resolution to the fight?

I raked my hands over my face and growled in frustration, the error of my choice hitting me like a ton of bricks.

Maybe I overreacted—I should have given her a chance to explain.

Maybe I read the situation wrong.

Fuck.

Did I fuck up?

My heart pounded in the cavity of my chest as I moved to reach for my phone on the nightstand, my fingers connecting with the smooth glass of the screen. I yanked it off the charger, nearly toppling over the jug of water that sat next to it. I sank down onto my bed, feverishly dialing her number. Listening to the ringing while I waited was torture.

Please pick up.

"Hey! This is Elle. Please leave a message..." I disconnected the call before hurling the phone across the room. It slammed into the wall, falling with a sharp thud on the floor.

I fucked up.

CHAPTER THIRTY

Elle

Cradling a steaming hot cup of coffee, I wrapped the blanket tighter around me and zoned out blankly on the roaring fire in my fireplace. It was nearing spring, but the chill throughout my body wouldn't dissipate no matter what method of warmth I tried. My body and mind were numb as I replayed over and over, every detail of that night at the bar. Our fight. His jealousy. The displaced trust.

The emptiness consumed me, leaving me feeling like a shell of the woman that I was. It was nearing two weeks, and while Ryder had called a million times, I wasn't ready to talk. Things with him had progressed so quickly, this felt like a wake up call.

I missed him.

But once again he had hurt me, whether or not he meant to.

The side of Matt that I had seen that night at the bar scared me. Perhaps I had read the situation wrong, and he was just being presumptuous because of our past fling, but I trusted my gut. The warning bells that sounded when he gripped my thigh were ones I wasn't willing to ignore, and instead of hearing me out and offering me solace after a moment that shook me, Ryder flew off the handle and assumed that I had been receptive of Matt's advances.

Spoiler alert: I hadn't been.

Not being given the opportunity to tell him my side is what hurt the most. At that moment, he didn't *care* about my side of the story and had just assumed the worst. It's one thing to be possessive and alpha-male, and I did truly enjoy that side of him, but it's a completely different thing to dismiss my feelings, thoughts, and *perspective*.

So as I sit here staring at the flames, I let myself think about what I truly want.

Him.

I want him.

But I didn't want that macho-caveman bullshit he pulled that night at the bar.

What if he didn't want me anymore? What if he decided that this wasn't worth it? That *I* wasn't worth it?

The thought made my stomach turn in unforgiving circles. I had done such a valiant job of giving myself time to process all of this; to stay levelheaded and true to myself, but for some reason I could feel myself falling apart under this blanket right now.

I needed my people.

Picking up my phone from beside me, I called Noah. The phone rang several times, pulling me further into my pity party with each ring. Finally, he answered.

"Hey," he said. "How are you?" I could hear the police scanner in the background. He must have been on duty.

"Been better," I told him truthfully. "Is now a bad time?"

"I have a minute. What's going on?"

"I just missed you. Wanted to say hi. How is everything with you?" I bit my tongue, knowing that he would be able to sniff out the lie in my voice. He always could. He also knew I was more of a texting kind of gal, so really I had set myself up for failure with this entire phone call.

"Cut the crap, Elle. What did he do?"

My head fell forward in defeat as I held the phone to my ear. I was internally arguing with myself about how much to tell him when the scanner went off in the background again. I waited until the dispatcher had finished talking before I opened my mouth to answer him, but I was cut off before I could.

"Elle, I'm really sorry, but I need to call you back. Will you be around later?" Noah sounded frustrated. But he was at work and that was more important than the problems that I was having, that I really shouldn't be talking to him about, anyway. Rosie would be better suited for this topic; I should have called her first.

"Of course, Noah. Be safe." Ending the call, I immediately scrolled to find Rosie's contact before pushing the call button. She was my crazy, tattooed therapist, and I knew she'd be able to pull me out of this funk. Thankfully, she answered on the second ring.

"Hey, ho! Let's go."

Her humor did little to cheer me up, and I rolled my eyes, even though I knew she couldn't see it. "Hey," I replied solemnly.

"Aww Elle, are you still feeling down? Why don't you just call the man and tell him to come fuck your brains out so you can feel better?"

"An orgasm isn't going to fix this, Rosie. He screwed up. I'm still so angry at him," I huffed, slumping down onto the couch farther.

The wind whipped through the speaker, muffling it slightly, and I could hear the sounds of cars passing. "He hasn't called?"

"No, he has, I just haven't answered," I told her.

"Babe, you can't work it out if you don't give him the chance to explain himself."

Rosie was giving me a small dose of her attitude. She was a no bullshit, work it out in the moment, kind of woman and with each day that had gone by that I hadn't spoken to Ryder, she was texting me updates on how she thought we were both being stupid.

"Like he didn't give *me* the chance to explain?" I was baiting her, finding myself looking for an argument for some reason, misplacing my anger.

"Valid point, but you have to remember he's a man, and men are idiots. Look, I'm not defending him by any means, but I know how long and how hard you fought to push the memory of him out of your life, and now you don't have to. I love that for you. I just want you to be happy." Her voice wavered and grew quiet. "I'm on team Elle, always, but maybe... just maybe... he deserves another shot with you? Don't forget the man was married for how many years? He probably has no idea how to navigate this new territory and these new feelings. Plus, it's been weeks. How long are you willing to let the silence stretch between you?"

I hated when she was right. I sat quietly, watching the flames dance and the embers fall on the bricks. "You're right," I whispered.

"Usually am." Rosie's voice was light, and it sounded like she had pulled away from the phone, distracted by something. "What did you say he does for a living again?"

"He owns a contracting business." This wasn't going the way I had planned. I needed to switch gears and pull myself away from the topic of Ryder. "Anyway, let's change the subject. What's going on with you? Want to come over for some wine?" I asked, knowing she would never turn down a wine night.

"Oh, you know, just a little this and a little that. Nothing special. You said his last name is Thompson?" Her voice changed its tone, full of darkness and mischief; a tone she only used when she was a woman on a mission.

"Uh ya, Thompson. Rosie, have you forgotten that I know you? I can hear it in your voice that you're doing something right now that you probably shouldn't be. Now, spill it."

Her laughter coursed through the speaker, a car door slamming in the background. "Hey, dickwad!" she bellowed, the sound of hammers and drills floating through to my end of the line.

"Hey! I'm talking to you, asshole," she continued to shout. My heart rate quickened.

"Rosie! Rosie, who are you yelling at?"

"Hang on, Elle," she told me sternly. I held my breath, straining to hear what was happening on her end of the phone.

"You. Yeah, you! Fucking. Asshole. What the hell are you thinking?!"

"Uh... what? Who are you?" I heard Ryder's gruff voice through the phone and my heart sunk so low in my stomach that I wasn't even sure it was still in my body.

"ROSIE, WHAT ARE YOU DOING!?" I screamed, desperate for her to return to our conversation.

This could not be my life right now.

"You know who I am, asshole. Now explain to me why you have been such a fucking coward that you'd rather sit in the corner with your tail between your legs instead of make up with the incredible woman whom you've been pining after for, oh I don't know, the last decade?!"

I began to sweat while Rosie continue to yell at Ryder, desperate to see the look on both of their faces, while also wishing this wasn't happening. I was embarrassed, but also proud of my best friend. She was a force to be reckoned with and when she loved; she loved fiercely. I was lucky enough to be a recipient of that love and her loyalty.

"I... uh..." Ryder's voice was low, clearly confused by the verbal assault he was receiving. I could picture him, brows furrowed as he rubbed the back of his neck.

"You... um..." she mock stuttered. "Come on, you fucking pussy, pull the dick out of your ass and go make up with the amazing woman you fucked up with. I wouldn't wait too much longer. She's a gem."

I put my phone on speaker, setting it in my lap and bringing my hands up to cover my face. The sound of gravel crunching signaled that Rosie was leaving, though she was silent on the other end of the line. I didn't dare utter the first word, too shocked to form a sentence, anyway.

"A treasure," Ryder's voice yelled from far off in the distance. Rosie's footsteps ceased.

"A what?" she called back to him, voice thick with attitude.

"I said she's a fucking treasure."

A moment later, a car door slammed. "He'll be in touch to make up. Love you, bitch," Rosie said, ending the call.

Laughter escaped my lips as I sat cross-legged on my couch, staring down at the blank screen of my phone.

That crazy bitch. Goddamn, I loved her.

CHAPTER THIRTY-ONE

Elle

When I finally pulled myself out of my own head, I decided that what I needed was a bottle of wine, some chocolate, and a hot bubble bath. I moved into the kitchen and opened the pantry, checking on my chocolate stash. Keeping a variety of chocolate and wine in the house was essential because, well, when is having chocolate and wine ever a bad thing? The chocolate was plentiful, but when I opened the refrigerator to pull out the bottle of pink Moscato that was chilling, it wasn't there. I stared into the cool abyss of the refrigerator, trying to remember when I had opened and drank the bottle, before remembering that Rosie had stopped by two nights ago and we shared it while sitting in the cozy patio chairs outside. Glaring at the refrigerator like my lack of wine was its fault, I slammed the door closed. Quickly I assessed my clothing—black yoga pants and an oversized, off the shoulder sweatshirt—and decided that was a good enough outfit for a quick jaunt to the grocery store down the street. I grabbed my keys, purse, and cell phone before locking up behind me.

I knew better than to grab a shopping cart when I entered

the grocery store, so I opted for a hand-basket. Making my way to the aisle which housed the wine, my eyes wandered over the labels until I spotted the sweet wines. From there, I quickly found my favorite brand and pulled two bottles from the shelf. Looking down at the bottles in my basket, I impulsively pulled a third from the shelf and placed it beside the two. Satisfied, I headed to the check-out stands, keeping my head down so that I wouldn't get distracted by all the tasty treats and end up with a mountain of groceries. I had one mission. Buy the wine, and that was it.

The woman at the check-out stand smiled maternally as she scanned the wine bottles and placed them into my reusable shopping tote.

"Rough day?" she asked, her voice sweet but raspy, sounding like she had been a smoker at one point in her life. I smiled back at her. She reminded me of my great aunt Janet.

"Rough couple of weeks."

"Been there honey, don't worry, it'll get better. Take these home and go relax in a bubble bath."

I threw my head back in laughter, beaming at the woman. Just in this short exchange, she was lightening my mood.

"How did you know that's exactly what I was going to do?"

Her eyes glinted with wisdom. "You think I don't know what frustration over a man looks like, sweet girl? Let me tell you a little something about men. If they're worth it, they're worth it. If they're not, run far and fast." She squinted and leaned forward slightly. I couldn't help but to follow suit and lean forward as well. "Is he worth it?"

I pursed my lips at her question, arms crossing over my chest. My face suddenly felt warm. I looked at her and bobbed my head in a nod. "Yeah, I think he's definitely worth it."

She handed me my receipt, her boney fingers overlapping mine as I reached to take it from her.

"Then make him work for it, baby doll."

I wrinkled my nose, laughter cascading from my lips once more. I shook my head, saying nothing as I grabbed my bag, cradling it from the bottom.

"You have a nice day, sugar."

"Thank you, ma'am. You too."

THE DRIVE HOME was quick and my wine sat shotgun as I belted out the lyrics to Lesley Gore's "You Don't Own Me," the music inspiring a little self-confidence. My decision to talk to Ryder and make him "work for it" solidified. I would talk to him tomorrow, but tonight was all about self-care—I had a date with myself and I intended on enjoying it to the fullest.

Approaching the four-way stop just before turning onto my street, I looked to the left to check for cars, before looking to the right. As soon as my head snapped in the direction of my house, the butterflies started swimming in my gut and my pulse quickened.

Ryder's truck was parked on the street.

I glanced at the clock on my dashboard, seeing that it was only a little after four in the afternoon.

He shouldn't even be off work right now, so why was he here?

Panic overtook my body as I sat idly at the stop sign. I wasn't ready to talk to him, not yet, not before I mentally hyped myself up for a potential argument, or worse, flat-out rejection. I couldn't do this, not now. The driver behind me tapped his horn in encouragement to go, pulling me out of my trance.

Instead of turning right, I turned left and continued driving *away* from my house. I had nowhere to go other than home, so I needed to think fast.

What would Rosie do? I channeled my inner baddie, my

inner *Rosie*, and slowed my car, hanging a U-turn in the middle of the street before slowing to a stop in front of a random house. Throwing the car in park, I killed the engine and sat in the silent car with only the sound of my rapidly beating heart to distract me. My eyes strained while I stared ahead at Ryder's truck, taking note of his head moving from within the cab.

He was sitting in his truck. Was he watching my house?

He obviously knew I wasn't there, so I could safely assume he was waiting for me to come back.

Well, I had news for him! I wouldn't be coming back anytime soon.

At least, not while he was there.

The angel and devil who loved to sit on my shoulders bickered for a while, my thoughts drifting between uncertainty and defiance. Maybe I should head over there and just hear him out. Listen to what he wanted to say. The angel pushed me to do just that, but the devil, oh that pesky little B, she dug her stiletto into my shoulder and forced me to stay put. I sighed, clicking the side button on my phone to check the time, realizing I had been sitting here for over twenty-five minutes. I was growing bored.

My eyes flicked over to the wine next to me and I quickly made a pros and cons list in my mind. Pros won, and I reached over to pluck a bottle from the grocery bag. Thank goodness I drink the cheap stuff and it had a twist top.

For two hours, I sat in my car watching Ryder watch for me, and drank wine straight from the bottle.

I had hit a new low. Slamming my forehead against the steering wheel in defeat, I winced, re-bruising the bruise that had barely healed from the last time. Keeping my head pushed against the steering wheel, I squeezed my eyes shut and once again debated with myself about just going home and facing Ryder tonight. I had polished off the bottle, so maybe with a little liquid courage, it wouldn't be so bad. We needed to work through this or say our goodbyes, but it was the goodbye part that had my stomach rolling and nerves increasing. I swallowed hard, my head lifting from the steering wheel, decision made to just rip the Band-Aid and go talk to him, but when my eyes came back into focus, Ryder was gone.

CHAPTER THIRTY-TWO

Ryder

I sat in front of Elle's house for almost three hours, like a goddamn stalker. The elderly woman who lived in the house in front of hers peered through the window countless times, doing her best to keep herself hidden from view. I'm surprised she didn't call the cops on me for loitering, or maybe she did, who knows.

I gave up and left once the streetlights came on and I realized she probably wasn't coming back any time soon. Pacing my empty condo, I thought about my next move and plan to get her back. Showing up at her house to talk hadn't worked, and my calls and texts still went unanswered. I was growing impatient, the insatiable need to see her—to touch her, growing more fiercely by the day.

This woman was going to be my undoing, and I needed to figure out a way to earn her forgiveness.

Now.

The ping from within my pocket stopped me in my tracks, and my heart did some fluttering shit as I reached for my phone. I growled, seeing Lily's name instead of Elle's.

LILY: Your son wants to talk to you. Is now a good time to call?

I rubbed the top of my head, clicking the call button to connect us.

"Hey, Dad!" Jordan said excitedly, answering on the first ring.

"Hey buddy, how are you? Mom said you wanted to talk to me."

"I'm good, and I do! I wanted to tell you that I got an A on my science fair project! The circuit board you helped me make was one of the most popular displays!"

"That's amazing buddy, I'm so happy for you. Did they give out any awards at the fair?"

"No, just the grades."

"Well, that's still awesome. How about we celebrate with milkshakes on Sunday?"

"Yeah! Can we get burgers too? And french fries, obviously."

"Obviously," I repeated, chuckling at my son. His appetite was hefty these days, and I knew from experience it was only going to get worse.

"Cool! Thanks Dad, here's Mom!" A sudden shuffle of noise pulled across the speaker before Lily's voice took over.

"He's literally insane," she told me, pride radiating through her words.

"I know. He's my kid, remember?"

"Yep, like father, like son." She laughed.

I didn't. My thoughts of Elle had taken over once again.

"What's wrong, Ryder?"

"Nothing."

"Have you forgotten that we were married for ten years? I know when you're in a shit mood, Ryder. What's up?"

"Nothing that concerns you, Lil. I don't want to talk to you about this."

She sighed dramatically, and I could practically see her eyes roll at me. "Okay, well, I'm here if you need to talk."

"Thanks. See you Sunday."

"Ryder?"

I inwardly groaned, raking a hand down my face. Sometimes she could be relentless. "Yeah, Lil?"

"Don't let her get away again."

I couldn't stop my mouth from falling open as she disconnected the call without waiting for me to respond.

She knew about me and Elle? How?

My pacing resumed as I slid my phone back into my pocket, hands coming up to clasp behind my head. Closing my eyes, I pushed myself to come up with a plan that would work.

Tomorrow was Friday—she'd be at work all day, and she couldn't hide from me there. A smile tugged at my lips as the wheels in my head turned, coming up with the perfect plan to win my girl back.

CHAPTER THIRTY-THREE

Ryder

Staring up at the office building that is home to *The Daily Reader*, I held my hand up to shield my eyes from the brightness of the sun reflecting off the mirrored windows. I blew out a breath, readying myself to begin my mission of winning Elle's forgiveness. This plan I had concocted will either be a make or break point for our relationship. If she rejects me after what I'm about to do, there would be no coming back from this for my pride.

Under any other circumstances, I would never willingly make a fool out of myself, but if Elle asked me to pluck the moon from the sky for her, I would figure out a way to do it. The level of insane that this woman made me was enough to have the most prestigious of therapists questioning if they knew how to do their job. My mind drifted back to the last few days and the emptiness I felt, and I could feel myself growing angry all over again. My hands curled into tight fists as I slammed my truck's door closed and trudged toward her office.

The lobby of the building was cool, both in temperature and in appearance. White and blue tiles lined the floor, a stark white reception desk sitting in the middle of the space while plush blue couches were offered for waiting guests. I continued toward the elevators, the receptionist standing to greet me. Her eyes widened when she took in the scowl on my face, watching as I slammed my finger on the up button by the elevator, waiting for the doors to open.

"Excuse me, sir?" Her voice was hesitant as she addressed me. "You need to check in sir, who are you here for?"

I ignored her, focused on the sound of the elevator doors opening. Stepping in without answering, I turned to read the list of businesses on the elevator's plaque, indicating that I needed to visit the sixth floor for *The Daily Reader.* I pressed the number six, watching through the closing doors as the receptionist rounded the corner of her desk to chase after me.

"Sir!" she called, just as the doors closed completely and I began my short ride to the sixth floor. My heart began to pound in my chest the higher the numbers climbed.

4...

5...

Ping.

The elevator leveled in its shaft and the doors opened, revealing a wall that read *The Daily Reader,* with yet another receptionist sitting in front of it.

She smiled brightly. "Hello, sir! Who are you here to see?"

Ignoring the woman, I moved around the wall, finding several cubicles with people pounding away at their computer keyboards. I followed the carpeted path between the desks, my eyes scanning for my dark-haired queen. It didn't take long for me to spot her from across the room, her desk caddy corner to a corner office with a wall of glass dividing it from the sea of cubicles.

Eyes snapped up from computers to focus on me as I weaved my way to Elle. A few women gasped, their eyes landing on me, and I received more than a few glares from the men, but my focus never wavered from where Elle sat. Her gaze was focused on the papers in front of her. She still hadn't noticed me approaching despite the room being so quiet that you could hear a pin drop, and many of her co-workers now standing behind their desks to see better. I stood behind her, my heart rate picking up as the smell of her perfume floated around me. I was desperate to reach out and pull her to me in a make-up kiss, but it wasn't the time yet.

"Elle."

She grew still at the sound of my voice, the paper in her hands free falling from her grasp and floating down to her desk. She spun slowly in her chair, her hand clutched onto the desk as if to steady herself.

"What are you doing here, Ryder?" she asked, her voice low. Her eyes bounced around the room, noticing that everyone was watching us intently.

"I've come to apologize and to beg for you back," I said matter-of-factly, my voice loud enough so that everyone around the office could hear. If I was going to make a public apology, I was going to make it a good one. "I screwed up, and I've been continuing to screw this up every day by letting the distance between us grow."

"Ryder now is not the ti—"

"No, Elle, now is exactly the time." I dropped to my knees and looked up at her. I lowered my voice so that the next words were hers, and hers alone. "I cannot go another minute without knowing that we're okay. I need to know that you are mine, because I'm fully fucking yours, Elle. I love you." Staring up into her eyes, I had never felt more sure of anything in my entire life, and the feeling made my heart inflate. "Now I'm going to say it in front of every fucker in this building." I tossed her a smirk before starting again, shouting this time. "I love Eloise Peters."

I could hear the distant "aww's" from around the office, but

I didn't dare pull my gaze away from her. She stared down at me, eyes hard. The seconds ticked by, feeling like an hour each as my eyes searched hers, pleading for her to give me a second chance. Hell, a third chance.

"Get up, Ryder," she finally said, pulling me by the bicep to encourage me to stand. I obeyed, allowing her to lead me back through the maze of cubicles and to the elevator. She pressed the down button, and we waited in painful silence until the doors opened, allowing us to step inside. Elle pressed the L for lobby and the doors began to close. She turned to me, finger poking me hard in the chest. "What the hell was that? Was that necessary to do in front of all of my co-workers, Ryder?"

I turned to the elevator's call buttons, my hand slamming into the emergency stop, jolting us to a halt in midair. Returning my gaze back to hers, I stalked toward her, forcing her to back up as my body invaded her space. Elle's breathing hitched, making me smirk, and her back hit the wall.

"I came here because you were avoiding me. You haven't returned my calls, my texts—I even showed up at your house and waited for you one night. I haven't heard from you in days, Elle. Almost *weeks*."

"I needed time to think."

"You needed time to come up with an excuse."

"I... that's not true."

"The hell it isn't. I know I scared you that night at the bar. I lost my temper and my jealousy consumed me. That's not me though, Elle, you know that."

"Do I though, Ryder? Do I know that? Because how well do we truly know each other? We were kids who never got to know each other and now, as adults, we jumped into the deep end headfirst and expected to know how to swim."

I reached up to tuck a piece of her hair behind her ears, my fingers grazing her cheek on the way down. "I know more about you than you probably realize, Elle. The big things and the small. I know that your favorite color is yellow, except with your favorite flowers, which are red roses. You bite your nails when you're nervous, and you look down at your feet when you're thinking. You hate cauliflower, love tacos, and your dream is to be running this entire fucking building. You love to read, write, and prefer sweet wine over anything else. You want two kids, a boy and a girl."

She stared at me in disbelief.

"Should I go on?" I whispered, pressing my forehead against hers.

"You..."

"When you talk, I listen. I remember the things you tell me, no matter how small. Because I love you, Elle. And I'm so fucking sorry."

Leaning down to kiss her, I began to stroke the seam of her mouth with my tongue, silently begging her to let me back in. The distance between us was beginning to shatter me. My heart sank further into my chest as she stood still, not yet returning my kiss. My fingertips swept up the side of her body before entangling in her hair. "Please kiss me," I whispered, forehead pressed against hers. "Please Elle, I can't let you go again."

My chest heaved with every breath, terror icing through my veins.

This was it.

I fucked up to the point where she wasn't willing to forgive me.

My eyes snapped shut, an unfamiliar sting suddenly burning them. A strangled breath caught in my throat when I felt her nose brush against mine.

"I'm going to make you work for this. You're not off the hook," she told me, her voice small.

Relief flooded through me and I crashed my lips into hers again, emotions flowing through me. I poured everything I had into that kiss, wanting her to *feel* everything I felt for her.

Without breaking apart, I wrapped both hands beneath her thighs and hoisted her up, encouraging her legs to wrap around me. I pushed her harder against the wall, tongue stroking hers. Her body melted into mine as I deepened the kiss, her fingers playing with the hair at the nape of my neck. I circled my hips, my hardened length rubbing against her center. I groaned, the friction making me desperate for more. Suddenly, everything felt right again.

"Um, hello? Is everything okay in there?" a timid male voice echoed through the elevator. I groaned, ripping my lips away from Elle to talk to the jerk who was ruining our moment.

"Everything is fine," I growled. "You can start the elevator."

No sooner had I finished my sentence, did my lips descend upon my girl's again, a whimper escaping her as I moved my hand to palm her breast. The elevator pinged, signaling the doors to open.

Without breaking our kiss, I moved her away from the wall and carried her through the lobby of the office building and out toward my truck. I kept her in my arms, my hand supporting her with a firm grip on her ass as I fumbled for the keys in my pocket. She nibbled on my ear, making it harder to concentrate on opening the door.

Once I pushed the key into the lock, I ripped the door open and dropped her on the bench seat, crawling over her and licking my way up her neck. She moaned, the sound connecting straight to my cock.

"Ryder, we can't do this here." Her plea was unconvincing, as my hand snuck beneath her shirt, skating up under her bra. Circling my thumb over her nipple, I played with it until it formed a stiff peak at my touch. My lips connected with her neck, suckling and licking my way to the soft flesh behind her ear. She shivered, eyes tightly shut, as she enjoyed my touch.

"Text your boss and tell him you're not coming back to work."

My hunger for her was raging. I moved to her mouth again, pushing my tongue inside and kissing her punishingly, grinding my cock against her center. She moaned into my mouth, her back arching as my fingers advanced past her stomach and connected with the hem of her skirt. I pushed it up enough to reach my hand underneath, my knuckles rubbing against the cotton of her panties. I could feel a wet spot soaked through the fabric and my cock grew achingly harder.

She panted beneath me, twisting her head to break our kiss. "I don't have my purse, Ryder. I only have an hour left. Just meet me at my house when I'm off work, okay?"

"Okay," I agreed, while licking her neck. "But first, you're going to come all over my fingers."

I gave her no further warning before plunging two digits into her and rolling my thumb over her clit. She rewarded me with a throaty moan and her nails biting into the forearm that was bracing me over her. I knew exactly what to do to make her come hard and fast and had no issues with using that to my advantage. There was no way I was letting her walk away without reminding her of exactly who she belonged to. She was mine.

I stretched her with my fingers, plunging knuckle deep as I worked her into a frenzy, loving the way she squirmed beneath me and suppressed a scream that I could tell was just begging to release from her throat. Dipping down, I tugged her bottom lip between my teeth before fully capturing her mouth, sucking her tongue into my own at the same time as I applied a little more pressure to her clit. Her walls clenched around my fingers, her back arching more than I thought possible considering she was pinned beneath me on the bench seat of my truck. A groan floated past my lips as I licked and nipped at her collarbone, my cock straining against my jeans.

"It's taking every ounce of restraint not to fuck you right now," I groaned into her soft skin, desperate to feel all of it against me. "I want nothing more than to feel you come all over my cock."

"You're so filthy," Elle told me as she pulled my head up level with hers and caught my lips again. Her arms wrapped around my neck, pulling me completely down on top of her as I continued to push her closer to her release.

Within seconds, she was coming for me and I had the pleasure of watching every bit of her climax dance across her face in the most beautiful way. I kept pumping my fingers in her, slowing my movements gradually as her orgasm released its hold on her. When her eyes finally opened, she beamed up at me, and my heart did a backflip at the sight. Her eyes were the bluest I had ever seen them, so much lighter than when her eyes had connected with mine upstairs. My heart tugged, knowing that I was the one who had dimmed her light. I would never, *ever*, fucking do that again. I removed my fingers from her and reluctantly pulled away, sliding down her body until my feet touched the ground. I adjusted my rock hard cock in my pants as she sat up, fixing her skirt and smoothing it.

"Okay, beautiful, back to work you go," I told her, leaning over and wrapping my arms around her body, sliding her toward me. She giggled as I extended my hand to help her down.

"Ever the white knight," she mused, hopping out of the truck.

"Maybe a dark prince is more suitable," I retorted, while kissing the top of her head. "I can't promise that I won't sometimes be the villain—the way I feel for you is beastly and there will be times where my jealousy fucks me up, but I will do my best to always be a knight for you."

Elle squeezed me tighter, the feeling of a nod pressing into my chest while I held her in the parking lot. My heart was finally feeling a little lighter knowing that she was still mine.

CHAPTER THIRTY-FOUR

Elle

I watched Ryder through my kitchen window while he lit the wood that was in my small outdoor fire pit. The flame began small, igniting first the piece of kindling before quickly catching, spreading to the smaller sticks and eventually the wood that we had doused in lighter fluid. My eyes were transfixed on the fire roaring to life and my lips hovered on the edge of my wineglass as I lost myself in my thoughts. I heard the door open and close, but I continued staring ahead, unable to pull my gaze away from the beautiful orange glow. My vision began to blur from my lack of blinking.

A pair of strong, warm arms snaked around my middle while pillowy lips kissed up my neck. "You ready to go sit by the fire, treasure?" he asked, hugging me tightly. His back rounded as he bent to rest his chin on my shoulder, staring out the window with me.

I smiled, turning my attention to Ryder. "Yeah," I told him, tilting my head to kiss his cheek.

He unwrapped himself from me before lacing his fingers through mine. Tugging me forward so we could make our way outside, he pulled the blanket off my couch when we passed by, and once outside, I curled up on the small outdoor love seat. He placed the blanket over my lap and I smiled at him as he pushed the edges beneath me, tucking me into a warm cocoon. After he was convinced that I was comfortable, Ryder sat down on the couch next to me, turning his body to face me.

I stared at the fire again, searching for the words to start our conversation, giving myself a moment before I spoke. "His name was Matt. I met him at a bar months before you came back into my life. We slept together once, that's it." My eyes zoned in on a pile of burning embers as I took a deep breath and continued on with my story. "The entire time I was with him, I envisioned you. Every relationship I have ever been in, I've never not wished it was you instead."

I looked over at him, then back down at my blanket, his gaze too heavy for me to continue to speak if I looked into his eyes.

"When you left for the restroom, he slid into your chair. He touched my thigh, and our entire conversation made me feel uncomfortable. I turned away from him to try and send the message that I wasn't interested, but it took him a few minutes to get the hint and leave. What you saw was me disregarding his advances, but you read into it all wrong. Then you didn't give me the opportunity to explain. I've been *so angry* at you because instead of giving me the benefit of the doubt, you jumped to all the wrong conclusions."

I stopped, bringing my gaze back to him, watching him. "You hurt me *again*, and I'm afraid that by letting you break down all of my walls, I could be nothing but a pile of rubble and ash at the end of this."

"There is no end of this." His voice was gruff, stare unwavering. "You are the endgame for me, Elle. There is no end of this—not for me."

"I want to trust you."

"You can."

"Can I though? How can I trust you with my heart if I can't trust you to trust my word?"

"I'll spend my whole life proving it to you, if that's what it takes. I don't care if it takes me until the day I die. I will prove to you that I won't fuck this up. Not again."

"But it can't be this simple. Your hesitance to trust *me* is what scares me the most, Ryder." My voice cracked, raw emotion seeping through. I could feel the tears slowly well up in my eyes, but I refused to let them fall.

"It can be that simple, Elle. You know what you mean to me—what you've always meant to me. I will never not trust you again. I fucked up, and I know that. I won't make the same mistake twice. I refuse to lose you."

He reached over to me, his large hand completely covering my small one. His fingers laced through the top of mine, pulling my hand to his chest. I could feel his heart beating, its pace matching with mine.

"Let me prove to you I can be the man you deserve." He pulled my hand to his lips, kissing my knuckles. "Let me show you that you're all I want in this life and the next."

Turning my attention back to the fire, I watched the flames dance and meld together, flickering and filling the air with its warmth, knowing with my heart that I couldn't be without him another day. I loved him and that love cut so deeply that the moments without him felt like I was bleeding out. The last few weeks had been hell, even worse than our ten years apart.

It was there, while watching the flames burn bright, that I let my heart guide me, reaffirming my decision to let him love me and to let myself love him.

"I love you, Ryder," I told him wholly, my eyes connecting with his green ones, giving him access to my soul. "I've loved you since I was a teenager. I buried that love deep inside of me for so long, but I never truly moved on from it. It's always been you. It'll always be you."

He pulled me into his arms, resting his forehead against mine. As my arms looped behind his neck, I stroked the soft hair at the nape of his neck and nuzzled into him, a sense of peace washing over me.

"I will never let you go again, Elle. Never. You're mine. You always have been. The piece of me that was always missing is finally whole, and it's whole because of *you*."

EPILOGUE

Ryder

The sun shined brightly over the horizon, its warmth radiating through the air as the guests of our wedding murmured quietly amongst themselves. They stole glances at me and my groomsmen standing in a tight row in front of the altar, while smiling brightly and taking in their surroundings. The venue was beautiful, much like the appearance of everyone around us, dressed to the nines. I had thought extensively of this moment, endless nights waiting to start our new chapter, and I couldn't believe this day had finally come—I was finally going to make her mine, officially.

Eloise Peters, soon to be Eloise Thompson. My wife. My fucking *wife*.

A smile overtook my entire face as I looked at my groomsmen, then again at our family and friends. I had never considered myself to be a sappy guy, but the amount of love radiating from the people around me was contagious. I had never known it could feel like this. Everywhere I looked, guests were talking animatedly, smiling from ear to ear, and buzzing with anticipation for the bride.

As I continued scanning over the sea of faces, I found Lily

and momentarily stilled as I caught her eyes running over the guests as well. She was searching, her face filled with anticipation, as though she was hoping for a certain face. I knew this look all too well; it was how I looked at Elle before she finally decided to be mine. It was a look loaded with hope and fear, lust and adoration. Without warning, Lily turned her head in my direction, and we stared at each other for a few moments. I smiled, and she smiled back, though I could tell her smile was a mask of sadness. My chest tightened because I knew exactly who she had been looking for, and I knew he wasn't here.

Although Noah was not present, I had to admit to myself that I was grateful for the bastard and what he meant to Elle. He had been a pillar in her life, protected her when I couldn't.

I could only hope he would be there for Lily too, assuming something was happening beneath the surface. Regardless of what may happen between them, Lily had come alive on her own, and I was glad to see her shine.

The music started up and Elle's bridesmaids began their descent down the aisle in their champagne-colored gowns, bouquets in their hands. Each took their place on the other side of the altar, hair and makeup perfect, warm smiles across their faces.

My eyes met Rosie's, and I was unsurprised that she was already looking at me with a flicker of attitude. A smug smile played at her lips, as if she knew exactly what I was thinking. If she hadn't shown up at my job site that day... well, I would like to think that I would have taken my head out of my ass and went to get my girl back, but I would be forever grateful that she asserted herself in my business—I just would never let Rosie know that.

Soft melodies of an acoustic "Clair de Lune" floated through the warm summer air and I turned my attention to where my bride would appear at any second. My breath hitched as she came into my line of sight, my eyes sweeping over her gorgeous body before locking with hers. She looked incredible; my pulse quickened as the sight of her coming toward me served as a reminder that this woman would always be mine.

My throat clogged with emotion while I watched her capture the attention of everyone around us. She peeked down at her brightly colored bouquet of wildflowers before looking back up at me. I was mesmerized by the siren in front of me. *My wife.* Almost.

Feeling a soft tug on the cuff of my sleeve, my eyes left Elle as I twisted my head to look at my son, my best man. Leaning into me, he whispered, "She looks beautiful, Dad."

I rubbed my hand over my smile, my heart beating wildly in my chest as I turned my attention back to my bride, before whispering back, "She absolutely does. She looks like the most beautiful treasure that has ever been found."

And she was mine.

Want More?

Continue reading for an
exclusive preview of
Lily & Noah's story

Wicked Games We Play

October 20, 2022

PROLOGUE

Noah

T he gold shine of my badge looked dull in the darkness as it bounced into the air when my fist connected with the table; everything on the dark cherry wood sent scattering in disarray. We have been playing this game on and off for over ten years, and I am growing tired of it. I am ready to take the queen—check fucking, mate. It's my turn to win.

I've always been sitting in the shadows, waiting. Watching her from afar and biding my time. Now, it's my turn.

She's mine.

She's always been mine, but I was man enough to know that before she could fully be mine, she had to be *his*.

I stepped aside, gave up the fight, and walked away from her the moment she told me she was pregnant.

The baby wasn't mine, and Lily was the type of girl—no, the type of *woman*, who was fiercely loyal. That ferocity amplified for the unborn fetus she had been carrying, and more so when her son was born. So for the last ten years I had been sitting idly and patiently waiting while she played house with *him*.

I have, of course, been asserting myself into her life from

time to time, always leaving the door cracked, but she never took the bait.

Like I said, she was fiercely loyal.

I knew 'til death do us part' was a vow she was unwilling to break, and I was a man of integrity. I would never actually want her to break that vow, but I still couldn't pull myself away from the memory of her, which made the temptation all too sweet.

As the thunder rolled viciously and the whiskey warmed my chest, I had found myself unable to resist the urge to ruffle her feathers.

What I wasn't expecting was the message that she sent back, ruffling mine more.

CHAPTER ONE

Lily

Taunting him was a game that I had become all too good at playing, although neither of us ended up being a winner when we played it.

Our game was frustrating, heart-wrenching, and wicked, but one I couldn't force myself to walk away from. He exhilarated me, made me feel like I was more than just someone's mother. He looked at me like I was his every fantasy, a thought that both lifted me up and broke me down.

I had spent years of my life with prickles of awareness coating my body, feeling that he was close by. I'd catch glimpses of him around the city, patrolling while on duty, looking impossibly gorgeous in his uniform. He'd ignore me, I'd ignore him, until one of us caved and texted the other. It was always innocent, until my divorce papers had been finalized.

Our game had never drifted over *that* line—I drew the line in the sand when I found out I was pregnant at seventeen. My high school boyfriend proposed out of obligation, and I had said yes, out of obligation. That was when I took the biggest stick I could and created the barrier between us: an invisible guardrail that kept me firmly in my lane and him in his.

And then my divorce happened nearly ten years later.

Suddenly there was a rift in the line, and I couldn't help but toe at the edge. It piqued my curiosity. I quickly learned that Noah was an easy man to rile up, and that I enjoyed the glint in his eye—the one that bordered on anger and lust. But if there was anything that I had learned after growing alongside of my child and being in a marriage of convenience for ten years, it was that I needed time to learn who I was.

My life had revolved around my son and my ex-husband for so long that I had no idea who *Lily* truly was. I was far past due on living my life and paving my own way in this world, and there was no way I was going to tie myself down to any man again so soon, regardless of how tempting he was.

He was determined to play for keeps, and I was determined to just *play*.

On the nights that my son was with his father, I intended on playing the field and enjoying what I had left of my twenties, which wasn't much, and maybe even experiencing what it was like to go through a 'hoe phase'.

If that 'hoe phase' included teasing a certain man who has always sparked my interest, then so be it. I was throwing the match into the gas tank and seeing how it exploded. I'd either get burned, or high on the adrenaline.

We did always enjoy our games.

Pulling my phone out of my pocket, I slid my thumb across the screen until I found his name. I stilled, contemplating my next move.

Looking down at my attire, I pursed my lips, deciding that

I could make what I was wearing work. Tugging on the hem of my v-neck tee shirt, I reached into the cup of my bra and pulled my breast up, before repeating the movement on the other side. The girls were now on full display, cleavage pushed together in just the right amount. I wasn't particularly busty, but I could work with what I had, especially with the help of Victoria's Secret push-up bras. Angling my phone downward and adjusting my body slightly to hide the pooch of my stomach, I snapped a photo of my breasts, analyzing it before clicking the send button. No text, just the photo—that was our current game.

We had been exchanging text messages here and there for several weeks; the content getting somewhat steamier as time went on. I couldn't deny the rush of adrenaline that hit every time I clicked send, and the anticipation that grew while I awaited his reply. Sometimes he only had me waiting a few seconds, while other times I waited days. So I did the same, matching him tit for tat.

The months that followed my divorce had been some of the most confusing, yet easiest, of my life. I had loved my husband, but I hadn't been in love with him for several years. We married out of obligation and although I had grown to love him, the fiery spark that I held for him before I got pregnant had been long gone.

He had been so adamant about doing the right thing by me and our son that I didn't fight him when he proposed. Instead, I gritted my teeth and watched my world spin out of control.

For ten long years, we stayed married, being each other's best friend and confidant, creating a beautiful life together. But that's all it was: friendship, partnership, roommates. Sure, we had sex somewhat regularly to soothe the need, but the passion that I craved from him never reignited between us. I struggled with my feelings for years before I finally admitted them to him. It was like something inside of me snapped that night. I could see the look in his eyes, the guilt because he had never let go of his longing for his *one that got away*, and if I was being honest with myself, neither had I.

Noah is my *one that got away*, but he is also the one that I am hesitant to let back in. I had caught a glimpse of who he was when we were both still in high school—temperamental, dominant, possessive, and authoritative—and although I love to read about those sexy alpha-males in my spicy books, I'm not so sure that having one in real life would be all that ideal.

Keeping him at arm's length was always what I intended to do, but he had somehow crawled under my skin the night I ran into him at the local watering hole, Andromeda. The memory from that night is still one that I get myself off too, more than I care to admit.

It was girls' night out and my other half, Alana, wanted to check out one of the newer bars in town. Jordan was with his dad, so I figured why not? I threw on my Spanx before slipping into my new bodycon dress. Self-doubt had washed over me as I turned side to side in the mirror, assessing my figure.

Over ten years since Jordan had been born, and my body still makes me self-conscious. I'm proud of my body and the tiger stripes that now adorned my stomach and thighs, but some days I couldn't fight the chokehold that my low self-esteem held me in, telling me I was too curvy and too fat. The logical side of my brain knew that just wasn't true, that my body was uniquely mine and beautiful regardless, but the insecurities crept in like a motherfucker sometimes.

I ended up deciding against the bodycon, pulling it down and let it pool at my feet while I stood in the middle of my closet, my eyes raking across the options. I selected a different dress, pulling it off the hanger instead.

The dress was beautiful, a white lace spaghetti strap that dipped low and gave me ample cleavage but flared to a loose sundress type fit just above the waistline. Beneath the lace was a nude underlay that clung to my body in a way that I wouldn't have to worry if the wind picked unexpectedly. Shoes were always the hardest with this dress, so I settled for a pair of strappy sandals. It was too casual for where we were going, but I also didn't care. It had been an unseasonably hot spring and I could wear what I wanted. Plus, it hid my mom body.

Mistake number one had been that stupid bodycon dress and how I felt when getting myself ready for the night. It should have been my first clue to just stay home and enjoy some self-care, but no, I had still continued on with my plans despite my downward self-confidence spiral.

Mistake number two had been *him*. I should have never let him do what he did that night, and it had been a domino effect ever since.

My body tingled as I felt eyes on me from across the bar. I looked around in bewilderment, wondering who I could be so acutely aware of, feeling my stomach flip with the idea of seeing him. We had been talking for weeks, but I was purposely keeping him at arm's length. My divorce was still too fresh. I wasn't ready for the door that I knew would open when I finally saw him.

There was no way he would be here tonight, but as my eyes swept the room, I knew that my gut was typically never wrong. I sucked in a sharp breath when I connected with the brightest pair of milk chocolate eyes. He wore a devious smirk as his eyes raked over my entire body, lingering slightly on my chest.

Noah was stunning. Dark brown hair that was cut short on the sides but left slightly longer on top, a trim beard covering his ruggedly handsome features. Just call me Beth Dutton, because there was a sexier version of Rip staring right at me.

He wore a black button down that was cuffed at the elbows and dark wash jeans, looking like sex and sin. I pulled my lower lip in by my teeth as I stood frozen in place, openly fantasizing over the demigod less than twenty feet away from me.

Every nerve ending in my body jolted to life as he made his way through the crowd and toward me, stopping toe to toe. He spared no second, gripping the back of my head and pulling me roughly, his mouth crashing into mine. The air escaped my lungs and forced my mouth to open against his. He stole my breath as his tongue found mine, encaging me in a punishing, dirty kiss. His grip tightened in my hair, the nip of pain mixed with pleasure he was awakening with his kiss.

He pulled me back by the hair, keeping my head close and rubbing his nose along mine.

"Hey, Lils." He chuckled darkly, leaning his forehead against mine.

I gripped the hair at the back of his neck, crashing my lips back to his. Years of hidden feelings came rushing to the surface as I held onto him for dear life, pouring every pent up bit of longing and lust into the kiss as I could. Noah lifted me by the back of my thighs and I wrapped my legs around his body as his hands slid to my backside. He began to walk with me in his arms. In that moment, I didn't care where we were heading, I only knew that this man would wreck me if I allowed him to. He had already begun peeling back my layers through his kiss.

He settled us against the wall of a dimly lit hallway and I took a moment to break the kiss, taking in my surroundings. The music from the bar carried into the space, but we were completely alone.

"How did you know I would be here tonight?" I asked, turning my attention back to him. He was licking his way up my neck, and I squirmed in his hold.

"I didn't. Right place, right time." He continued nipping at my neck as his fingers bit into my thighs. Placing me on my feet, he pulled back, looking at me in the eyes. "I've waited so long to taste you."

"So taste me. Let me taste you." I moved to capture his lips and traced my tongue along his bottom lip, snaring him in a slower kiss.

His hand trailed along my side before he moved it back to my hair, circling my blonde curls around his fist. We kissed for several minutes, making out like teenagers who had snuck off between classes. The feeling brought me back to high school, making me long for the kiss I never got from him back then. A noise sounding like a cross between a moan and a whimper escaped me, my heart aching for the missed opportunities of the past. He pulled away, searching my eyes for the source of the sudden sadness.

"We have the rest of our lives to make up for lost time, Lils."

I shook my head. I wasn't ready for that.

"No, it's too soon. I've told you that, Noah. I need time on my own."

His eyes darkened, and he hesitated before grabbing onto the hem of my dress.

"Fine, but let me at least taste you now," he growled, dropping to his knees in front of me. My breathing hitched as he lifted the lace of my dress and I realized what he was doing. He bunched the lace up and forced my hand to wrap around it, holding it up as he slid the underlay up my body. I watched his brows come together in confusion when he was met by the unattractive nude layer of my Spanx. "What the fuck are these?"

I laughed, watching him as he reached into his back pocket. My eyes widened when he pulled a pocketknife out, exposing the sharp blade with the flick of his wrist.

"Stay still."

I held my breath as he ran the blade along the side of my Spanx, destroying one side before moving onto the other. He pulled the ruined fabric away from my body, tossing it behind him. A shiver ran through me as he ran the cold, smooth blade down the inside of my thigh before folding it and sliding it back into his pocket.

He licked his lips, eyes trailing along the lower half of my body.

"Do you have any idea how long I've pictured seeing you like this?"

"You've seen plenty, we've been playing our texting game for weeks."

He looked up at me, situating back. "You know that's not the same."

"*I know.*"

He hooked his finger through the thin fabric of my panties that rested on my lower belly. The proximity heated my cheeks and I was suddenly all too aware that my lower half was fully on display, including my stomach. I blew out a breath, begging my self-consciousness to crawl back into the hole where it came from. It was ruining the moment.

"*I want to taste you now, Lily. Tell me I can.*"

A war brewed inside me, but arousal took over the second his teeth raked against the fabric that rested on my lower belly. A fire roared to life within me, and I suddenly wanted nothing more than to be touched by this man. I nodded my head yes, giving him permission.

"*I need your words. Say it, Lily.*"

"*Yes. Please, yes,*" *I whimpered. He ripped the panties down my legs, using the fingers he still had woven around them to remove them from my body. Lifting my leg, he draped it over his shoulder and dove against my center, sliding his tongue through my slit.*

My head slammed against the wall in pleasure as he devoured me, pulling pleasure from my body hard and fast. I was writhing against the wall, a slur of praise and curses tumbling from my lips as alternated between circling my clit and spearing me with his tongue. I was dizzy with lust, shamelessly riding his face in the middle of a dimly lit hallway, somewhere in the back of a completely packed bar. Fisting his hair in my hands, I was desperate to hold onto something as I was driven to the brink of my orgasm.

Feeling that I was close, he inserted his finger into me, swirling around my desire before adding another. The combination of his tongue with the friction of his fingers was too much and sent my body into overdrive as my orgasm crashed into me. I screamed out his name, chasing the high as he relentlessly drove his fingers into me, my body clenching around them while he pulled every last drop of my orgasm from my body. My body went limp as he removed his fingers from me, pulling my dress down as he stood. He grabbed my chin with his hand and pressed his lips to mine, capturing me in another dirty kiss.

The taste of me on his tongue jolted me to reality.

Needing to catch my breath, I turned my face, forcing myself to not freak out.

Noah dropped his hand before lacing his fingers through mine, lifting it to his mouth to kiss the top of my hand.

"I'm still waiting, Lily. As long as it takes."

WICKED GAMES WE PLAY
OCTOBER 20, 2022
preorder now

ACKNOWLEDGMENTS

Thank you so much for reading debut novel, Between the Flames! I hope you loved getting to know these characters and that you will check out the upcoming books in this series of Ridgewood stand-alones. I still can't believe I wrote a freaking book.

I'd like to give some very special 'thank you's' to everyone who helped me make this book possible.

Amanda, Rana, April, Athena, and Theresa, thank you for being the first sets of eyes to ever read my words and for helping me shape this book. I love you all so much and appreciate you.

Nicole, Chelsey, Bethany, and Paula, thank you for being the second sets of eyes and for all the helpful feedback, you guys are the best.

Thank you to my incredible editor, Virginia, and my fabulous proofreaders, Nicole and Kaitlin.

To my amazing street team, my Smut Ducks, thank you for literally being the best cheerleaders ever. Seriously, I adore every single one of you.

The *biggest* thank you to my husband and parents for always believing in me and standing by my side throughout every path I've ever wandered down. Even though I really don't want you to ever read my books, I will always acknowledge you in them because without you guys, I don't know where I would be in life.

And finally, thank you to all of my book besties on Book-Tok. The support you all have given me throughout this process has been nothing short of incredible.

ABOUT THE AUTHOR

A.R. Rose is a wife, mom, reader, and writer, who lives in sunny California with her family and two dogs. She loves to hang out at home, drink copious amounts of coffee, and eat yummy food

90% of the time you will find her with a book or her Kindle in hand, reading a spicy romance novel, which not so coincidentally is what she has fallen in love with writing.

CONNECT

Join A.R. Rose's newsletter for exclusive info & updates
♥https://bit.ly/arrosenewsletter

Website
♥www.authorarrose.com

Reading Group
♥https://www.facebook.com/groups/authorarrose

Facebook
♥https://www.facebook.com/authorarrose

TikTok
♥https://www.tiktok.com/@authorarrose
♥https://www.tiktok.com/@alexreadsromance

Instagram
♥ https://www.instagram.com/authorarrose

CPSIA information can be obtained
at www.ICGtesting.com
Printed in the USA
BVHW031015100822
644276BV00010B/201